CLAIMED BY THE BEAR KING

JESSICA GRAYSON

ARIA WINTER

Purple Fall
Publishing

DEDICATION

To my husband: You are not just my husband, you are my best friend and my rock. Thank you for all your love and support. I love you more than words can ever say.

-Jessica Grayson

CHAPTER 1

ANNA

The winter moon shines brightly overhead. Silver light filters through the snow-covered trees, draping the world around me in an ethereal glow. If not for the fear in my heart, I would think it beautiful. Smoothing my hands down the white, fur-lined gown of my wedding dress, I clasp them tightly together in front of me to still their trembling. I always thought my marriage would be to someone I love, not to a stranger.

The man who will be my husband walks toward me. King Henrick—the Bear Shifter king of the North—is just as fierce as I have heard. Dressed in heavy armor, he appears more ready for battle than marriage. With his right hand on the hilt of his sword, his ice-cold gaze studies my father at my side as if suspecting he will attack at any moment and save me from this wedding.

What he does not realize is that my father is a coward. He traded his only daughter to his enemy, and he will not go back on his word now. Not when he may keep his kingdom and the wealth he was paid in exchange for my hand.

The silver light of the moon casts just enough illumination I'm able to make out the king's features. He has short, blond hair so pale it is almost white. He is so tall, the top of my head is barely level with his chin. His ice-blue eyes fix upon mine intently, his expression severe, reinforced by a strong square jaw that could cut glass. His shoulders are broad, and beneath his armor, he has a warrior's build.

Thick cords of muscle line his arms, flexing as he extends his hands toward me. I tip up my chin, forcing myself to meet his intimidating gaze as I place my shaking palms in his. He is more muscular than any man I've ever seen, but I suppose I should have expected no less from the fierce Bear Shifter king of Arnafell.

He is known far and wide for his sharp, calculating mind and his prowess in battle. My father underestimated him when he tried to invade Henrick's lands. Now I am the one paying the price for his foolish mistake.

King Henrick's eyes drop to my trembling hands. He glances toward my father then returns his intense gaze to me. "Tell me. Do you stand here today of your own accord?" His voice is deep and bordering on thunderous.

When I do not answer immediately, his lips pull back in a feral snarl, baring his sharp fangs at my father.

Drawing in a deep breath, I steel myself and squeeze his hands. His head snaps to me. "Yes, my lord. I am here of my own volition."

His ice-blue eyes search mine for a moment before he dips his chin in a firm nod and turns to the High Priest. "You may proceed."

We recite our sacred vows beneath the light of the winter moon. Each word passing my lips fills me with dread, binding me to this man—this conqueror who stands before me.

My mother sheds silent tears, clinging to my older brother. Han's expression is pained while he watches my father give me away to our enemy.

The High Priest surveys the small crowd that has gathered. "Are there any who protest this marriage?"

My brother's hand goes to the hilt of his sword, and my eyes widen. I give him a subtle shake of my head and mouth the word *no*.

Mother places her hand over his, pulling it away from the weapon at his side. A single tear slides down my brother's cheek as his eyes hold mine. "Forgive me," he whispers.

Unable to speak through my emotions, I nod. There is nothing to forgive. This is Father's doing, not his.

After the binding words are spoken, my husband holds his arm out to me, and I loop mine through. Together, we walk toward the dining hall for the celebratory feast.

I keep my eyes trained on the castle ahead. A blanket of snow covers the normally green fields surrounding the high walls. This place used to be my sanctuary—a refuge of safety and warmth.

Peering up at King Henrick, dread fills me anew. Tonight, there will be no rest; no rescue from what is expected of a new bride and her husband. I swallow against the knot in my throat and blink back my tears.

I pray that he is at least gentle. I've known no man before him.

The dining hall is decorated in the banners of ice-blue and silver with the sigil of the white bear in the center—the banner of Henrick's Kingdom of Arnafell.

My Kingdom, now, as well.

It's strange to think I will be leaving the Kingdom of Ered

tomorrow. I have never even travelled outside of its borders before.

The servants guide us to a table along the far wall overlooking all the others. Henrick and I sit directly at the center.

Plates overflowing with meat, cheese, fruits, and bread are laid out before us, along with tall, fluted glasses of champagne.

Normally, I avoid the drink. Especially since I've seen what it does to my father. However, as I watch my husband ravenously eating from his plate, I down one glass, then another, praying it will dull the pain I've heard may come from the first joining.

We sit side by side in awkward silence. I can hardly believe that by the time the sun rises in the morning, I'll have been thoroughly claimed by this man. I curl one hand into a fist, pressing it into my lap to still its shaking, and take another glass of champagne.

My father, rising and commanding everyone's attention, introduces the dancers who will entertain us for the night, but Henrick wants none of it. My new husband stands from his chair, and the crowd falls silent as he extends his hand to me.

Cautiously, I take it, and he pulls me up beside him before turning a hard glower on our guests. "My queen and I will retire for the evening."

Queen.

There was a time, not long ago, when I dreamed of being called that. But hearing the word fall from the mouth of my severe husband sends a tremor of fear straight down my spine. He is claiming me as his before our guests, and now we go to consummate our union.

My father snaps his fingers, and several servants appear to guide us to our chambers for the evening.

Following them down the long hallways of the guest

wing, I struggle to push down my fear, holding my head high. I focus on calming my pounding heart and rapid breathing.

I know I'm not the first woman to be married against her wishes, and I certainly will not be the last. My mother went through this with my father.

If others can endure it, so can I.

When they lead us to separate anterooms, Henrick growls a warning. "Why do you separate us?"

One of the servants stops and bows. "My lord, it is to prepare you both for your joining. I assure you, you will be reunited shortly."

He turns to me. "Is this how it is done according to your traditions?"

Shakily, I nod. "Yes, my lord."

He tells the servant, "Proceed."

She leads him into one room and me into another.

My body trembles as I'm guided into a warm tub of water. I feel numb, staring straight ahead, while servants move the washcloth across my shoulders and back.

When I step out of the tub, my ladies-in-waiting dry my body and my long, chestnut hair until it flows past my shoulders in glossy waves. They dress me in the silken gown of joining. The material hides nothing of my form, and for the first time, I wonder why my people even bother with such a ridiculous covering.

Once I'm dressed, they guide me into the bedroom then leave. I view the large, four-poster bed beside me, the thick white comforter pulled back to reveal stark-white sheets— no doubt, for the benefit of my new husband, to assure him that before our joining I was untouched.

Fear trickles down my spine when I hear the latch of the door click. My head snaps toward the sound, and I watch my husband step inside.

JESSICA GRAYSON & ARIA WINTER

His ice-blue eyes are hungry as they travel up and down my body.

Hard planes of muscle lining his chest and abdomen peek through the similar sheer robe he wears. My focus wanders farther down, and my mouth drifts open at the sight of his manhood, hard, erect, and straining against the confines of his clothing as he strides toward me.

He is much larger than I imagined he would be and I worry that our joining will be painful.

When he reaches me, he removes his robe then unfastens mine with sure and eager hands. He pushes the fabric back from my shoulders, and it falls to the floor, pooling around my feet.

His intense gaze holds mine as he reaches out to touch my cheek. His thumb traces across my lower lip before he slides his hands down the column of my neck to the valley between my breasts. I inhale sharply as he cups my breast in his palm, and the peak hardens into a stiff bead.

My heart hammers as he dips his head to the curve of my shoulder, scenting my neck. "You are mine," he growls.

CHAPTER 2

HENRICK

Even now, I struggle to hide my reaction behind a stoic mask when her hazel eyes meet mine. Anna's face is as familiar to me as my own. I have seen her almost every night in my dreams, ever since the blood witch —the Snow Queen—placed a curse upon my heart so I could never love.

Studying her features, I'm spellbound.

Has she ever dreamed about me, I wonder.

To dream of one's mate and find them is the greatest blessing that can be bestowed by the gods. I cannot imagine what I have done to deserve such a gift, but I also know better than to question it.

Anna is the most beautiful female I have ever seen. Long, silken hair frames her lovely heart-shaped face, her features so delicate I worry for a moment she may be hurt during our joining.

She is completely bare before me. Her hazel eyes watch me as I reach forward and touch her cheek, admiring the warm blush that follows. I run the pad of my thumb across her full bottom lip, wondering what it would be like to kiss her.

Her pale skin is petal-soft beneath my callused fingers. I trace them down the elegant column of her neck to the valley of her breasts. She gasps as I cup one soft globe in my hand and brush my thumb over the peak. It forms into a hard bead, as if begging for my attention.

I dip my head to the curve of her neck and shoulder, skimming the tip of my nose along her delicate flesh and drawing her essence deep into my lungs, memorizing the scent of my mate.

My *stav* is hard and straining with desire to join my body to hers. A bead of liquid gathers on the end, and I do not want to wait any longer. I gather her into my arms and walk her to the bed, laying her gently beneath the covers.

My need is so great I can barely contain it. I crawl over her. She parts her legs, and I settle between them. My chest rumbles as the tip of my stav bumps her entrance.

She inhales sharply, and my nostrils flare, the acrid scent of her fear permeating the air. I frown, searching her eyes. "Are you afraid of me?"

She blinks up at me, and in her face, I already recognize her answer. A tear slips down her cheek.

She is terrified.

I move off her and turn onto my side, studying her intently. I smelled her fear during the wedding, even during the banquet, but I believed it was because I had yet to claim her.

Female Bear Shifters are anxious after a bonding. The ceremony is quickly followed by the consummation and claiming to dissuade any unbonded males from challenging the one she chose for the right to become her mate.

That is why I made us leave the reception early. I wanted

to claim her before any other male would dare think to challenge me, and I meant to gift her mind the ease of knowing I had not changed mine.

But staring down at her now, it seems I was wrong. Humans must not share this custom.

"Yes," she whispers so low I almost miss it.

I swallow against the bile rising in my throat as she eyes me like I'm some sort of monster here to take her against her will.

Clenching my jaw, I sit on the edge of the bed, turning my back on her and running a hand roughly through my short, blond hair. "You need not fear me. I would never force myself upon you."

I stand from the bed, drag a blanket and pillow off the top of the mattress, and head for the door.

"Where are you going?" Her small voice rings behind me.

I drop the bedding just inside the door and turn to face her. "I will not come to your bed until you ask me to."

Her small brow furrows, her hazel eyes searching mine for a moment before she ventures, "What if I never do?"

Her words hit me like a physical blow. I married her to produce heirs. My kingdom will not be secure without them. However, if we mate, it must not be my choice alone. I clench my jaw. "Then so be it."

Her mouth drifts open as she blinks across at me.

I turn away from her and settle on the floor, pulling the blanket over my shoulder and closing my eyes. Sighing heavily, I will my body to calm as I try to drift off to sleep.

Despite my efforts to relax, my stav is still painfully erect. I hear the soft pad of her approaching footsteps. As much as I wish to see what she is doing, I dare not turn around. I do not wish to scare her, for I am certain hunger still shines in my expression.

I hear the light rustle of clothing and realize she must be

gathering her gown off the floor. A short huff of air escapes me.

What good does it do to cover herself? The material hides nothing of her body. I've never seen a more ridiculous item of clothing.

Yet if the illusion of cover gives her comfort, so be it. I will not gaze upon her nude form without her permission.

It occurs to me I could easily release her from our marriage. I could leave to speak with her father right now, give her back to him, dissolve our bond, and be on my way.

When I agreed to the marriage, I did so believing it was her wish, as well.

Now, I am uncertain.

Anna may not desire me now, but I realize I cannot let her go. She is my Fated One. Of this, I am certain. The gods brought us together, and I know without a doubt she is linked to my destiny and my curse. I must understand why.

CHAPTER 3

ANNA

Henrick falls asleep on the ground by the door. I pull my sheer robe back over my shoulders, slipping back into the bed and tucking the comforter tightly around me. With his back turned to me, I take a moment to study my new husband.

His reaction to my fear shocked me.

Perhaps he is not the monster I heard he was.

As I scan his broad, muscular shoulders, I cannot deny he is an attractive man. However, I'm also still afraid. He said he would not come to my bed until I asked, but I wonder whether his patience will run out.

As I observe Henrick, I pray that we can come to some kind of understanding. Until we consummate the marriage, it can potentially be annulled, then we can go our separate ways.

Closing my eyes, I send a silent prayer to the gods that this could be so. I cannot imagine staying married to this man, nor that he'd wish to remain married to a woman who will not warm his bed.

When morning comes, I find Henrick already awake and dressed. He is standing by the window, surveying the city below.

I remain quiet, studying him a moment.

Sensing my gaze upon him, he speaks. "I have heard snow is rare here in the Kingdom of Ered."

I sit up, pulling the blanket with me to cover myself. "It is, my lord."

His eyes sweep to me. "You must be sure to pack warm clothing. It is always cold and snowing in Arnafell."

My heart stutters and stops. "You—you still wish to take me with you?"

He frowns. "You are my queen."

"But I—" My gaze drops to the bed. "We did not consummate our marriage. I thought you'd wish to be released from our bonding. That we might annul our arrangement."

"I bound myself to you beneath the winter moon and the gods above," he says as if that settles the matter.

"You still want me as your queen?"

"Yes," he replies matter-of-factly.

"Even though I may not share your bed," I repeat, just to be sure.

"After we have spent more time together, you will get used to me."

"*Used* to you?"

"Like a horse that must be gentled."

My jaw drops as indignation rears. "I am *no* horse."

"Of course not, but the idea is the same. You will remain

in my presence at all times. Eventually, you will grow used to me. At ease, even."

I open my mouth to speak, but the words won't come. I've never been addressed so rudely before.

What kind of man have I married?

"Are you packed and ready for travel?"

I blink at him. Still stunned, I barely manage to reply, "Yes."

"Good. We will leave now."

"But… my mother, my brother… I must say goodbye to them."

A hint of irritation shifts into his expression. "I will send for them to meet us outside. We cannot delay long." He glances back at the window and the sky beyond. "A heavy snowstorm brews to the north. If we wish to stay ahead of the storm front, we must leave soon."

"I… haven't even had breakfast," I tell him, trying to stall.

His brow furrows. "Then you will eat along the way. We will not stop until we reach the village of Islo."

"Islo?" I blurt incredulously. "That's at least a day's ride from here."

"Which is why we must leave now," he repeats. He opens the door and steps into the hallway, calling over his shoulder, "I will be downstairs waiting. Do not take long."

As soon as he's gone, I call for my ladies-in-waiting. They hastily help me dress while my father's guards take my trunk with all my belongings downstairs.

When I step into the courtyard, true to his word, Henrick has already summoned my family.

Flakes of snow twirl on the breeze, falling softly upon the ground. It rarely gets cold enough for such weather, and my brother and I used to be so excited every time it would snow.

Now, I can feel nothing but dread as I observe the light snowfall all around me.

As I glance at my new husband and think of where we are going, I realize just how much I'll miss the warmth of my father's kingdom.

My mother, my father, and Hans are all standing nearby. I frown when I do not see any carriages. Perhaps they're not ready yet.

I wonder how many carriages and horses the Northerners brought. After all, I did not see Henrick arrive last night before the ceremony. I only saw him in the woods when we said our vows.

The guards carrying my trunk seem confused. They consult one of Henrick's men. "Where should we place this?"

In a whirl of dust and wind, I watch Henrick's guard transform before my eyes into a hulking bear covered in snow-white fur. I have seen many bears before, but never any this big.

My family's eyes are wide, watching him secure the strapping to his middle and instructing my father's guards to arrange the trunk on his back.

I turn to my mother, and she hugs me tightly to her chest. My brother joins us, whispering in my ear, "I won't let you leave."

I pull back just enough to meet his tear-brimming eyes. "You must, Hans."

"I'll fight for you."

I shake my head. "No. You would be killed. You must stay here so you can someday lead our people—be the ruler our father could never be." I pause. "Besides… the Bear King is not as cruel as we've heard."

Mother's brow furrows. "He was gentle last night when you consummated the marriage?"

My cheeks heat at her question, embarrassed she would ask about that, especially in front of my brother. "Nothing happened. He said we will wait until I am ready." I meet their eyes evenly. "I am not afraid to go with him. Not anymore."

It is a half-truth. I still have fears, but not nearly as many as I did before last night.

Mother's jaw drops.

Though a muscle ticks in his jaw, my brother nods. "If you need me, send word. I will defy Father and come for you if you change your mind."

A faint smile tips my lips up at his words, for I know he speaks truth. Hans would wage war for me, no matter the cost to our kingdom or the orders of our father. I hug him tightly once more then turn back to Henrick.

His icy gaze practically bores into mine. I glance at my ladies-in-waiting. "Is the carriage coming for me and my ladies?"

He frowns. "Your handmaidens are not coming with us."

"What?" Tears threaten to come as I turn back to Engrid, noticing sadness mirrored in her pale green eyes. "But I—"

With a scowl of irritation, he turns to one of his men. Something unspoken passes between them, and he turns back to me. "Your handmaidens are important to you?"

I straighten. "Yes."

"Choose one."

"I—" Words escape me. I half expected him to argue with me that no one could go. Without hesitation, I turn to Engrid. Of all my ladies-in-waiting, she is the one I also consider my friend and confidante. "Engrid will come with me."

I turn back to Henrick, about to thank him, but he cuts me off by transforming into a bear even larger than the one standing beside him. My heart hammers in my chest at his approach.

Ice-blue irises study me as his pupils contract and

expand. Snow-white fur covers his entire body. Sharp, black, lethal claws scrape the snow as he moves toward me.

Unable to stop myself, I reach a trembling hand toward his face, sliding my fingers through the fur along his jaw while he stares at me intently.

"Are you ready to leave?" he asks, his words thick as they form around two rows of sharp fangs.

"Yes." He crouches and regards me expectantly. "You... want me to ride on your back?"

"Unless you'd prefer to walk."

Drawing in a deep breath, I move to his side. Gripping his fur tightly, I manage to pull myself up onto his back. Because of my dress, I have to sit with my legs on one side.

He glances over his shoulder. "You will fall that way. You must straddle me."

"I will not." It is not befitting a woman of noble blood to ride in such a way. "I assure you I'm an excellent rider; I will not fall."

It occurs to me that I'm speaking as though I'm riding a mere horse, not my Bear-Shifter husband.

He huffs out a frustrated breath. "Fine." I tip my chin up. "For now," he grumbles.

"What do you—"

He stands, and a surprised yelp escapes me as I nearly tumble over the side.

He glances back at me, and I quickly regain my composure. I refuse to meet his eyes and see the judgment I know I will most certainly find there.

His ribcage expands beneath me with a heavy sigh as he turns to his guards. Each has shifted into his bear form behind us.

Engrid's eyes are wide when they meet mine. She sits atop one of the guards, both legs on one side just like me. She offers me a faint smile, and I nod, trying to appear calmer than I feel at this moment.

My heart hammers in my chest as Henrick begins to walk, his powerful muscles rippling beneath me, reminding me my husband is not just a man. He is a fierce and powerful Bear Shifter.

My father's guards pale as they observe us pass, and not for the first time, I wonder if I've made the right choice.

CHAPTER 4

HENRICK

My mate is very stubborn. I am concerned she will fall, but she insists upon riding in this ridiculous fashion, with her legs on one side. I am aware that noblewomen are expected to do such things, but I would never require this of my bride. Especially, when it could compromise her safety.

It is highly impractical and dangerous, and I worry she will tumble off my back and injure herself.

As I glance back at her, she tips up her chin in defiance, refusing to meet my gaze.

I sigh heavily at her dismissal of my concern for her safety. I suspect she is stubborn and determined enough to keep such a thing as falling from happening.

Perhaps this is good; a sign I have chosen well. My mate is strong-willed and determined. Hopefully, our children will inherit this strength from her.

That she is comfortable enough to disagree with me is progress. Already, she is growing accustomed to my pres-

JESSICA GRAYSON & ARIA WINTER

ence. She knows I will not harm her. Now, I must do all that I can to assure her that I will be a good mate and provide for all her needs.

There is only one thing that I cannot give her. I can never truly love her. My curse—the ice around my heart—will prevent it. Always. I do not know of any way to reverse it. I have tried many times, but to no avail.

It should not matter, however. I have seen enough of marriage to know that love is not the cornerstone of such a relationship. Respect and understanding are. I witnessed this with my own grandparents. I expect it will be the same with Anna and me.

As we start away from the kingdom, several people line the cobbled streets to bid their princess goodbye. I notice many mournful gazes as we pass, but I do not understand why. She is a queen now. Our kingdom is much larger and more powerful than this one. Surely, they see that she has married well. In addition to that, our marriage has secured a lasting peace between our people.

I feel her shift above me and I glance back to see her waving at the crowd, a smile plastered on her face. She jostles slightly, nearly losing her balance, and I growl. "Hold on to me with both hands," I insist.

With the smile still bright upon her face, she turns to me. Her eyes widen a moment before she speaks through her teeth. "I cannot."

"You will fall."

"And you are likely to be murdered before we even leave this kingdom if it looks as though I am anything but the happy and blushing new bride, *dear husband.*"

Although I have heard women refer to their mates with this particular term of endearment when they are happy with their spouse, the way she says it suggests she is annoyed instead of pleased.

"Killed?" I ask under my breath.

"Yes," she replies in a voice so low I almost miss it. "You forget that I am their beloved princess and you are the king who conquered our lands. And now you're taking me away. How do you think this looks to them?"

My brow furrows deeply. "Like we married to secure peace between Ered and Arnafell."

I surmise this is the wrong answer as she gives me a saccharine smile and leans down to whisper in my ear. "Do you not see some of the men in the crowd? They are still angry that they were beaten by your forces. Their pride has been wounded. If they believe I am unhappy, they might try to regain some of it, by being the hero that saves me from my husband—the conqueror."

She is right. That is why I agreed to this marriage when her father offered her hand. I wanted to avoid any further border skirmishes and bloodshed.

As I dart a glance around the crowd, I doubt any of these men could actually kill me if they tried. I am a very hard male to kill. Especially in this form. However, I do not wish for them to consider me their enemy. Not anymore.

I look back at my mate and my chest swells with pride as she continues to smile and wave at the people lined up along our procession. I have chosen it well, it seems. My mate is as intelligent as she is beautiful.

More importantly, it seems she does, at least, care for me enough to not want me killed.

She turns to me and speaks through her teeth again. "Do try to walk slowly and carefully. It would not do for me to fall while we're walking amongst the people."

I give her a pointed look. "Then, perhaps you should ride as I've suggested. It would be safer that way and—"

"Not befitting a queen," she says, cutting me off.

Last night, she was afraid, and it worried me to know that

my mate feared I might harm her. But today, she is flexing her claws as she argues with me. It pleases me that she is comfortable enough to argue her point, knowing that I would never hurt her, but I hate that she compromises her safety for the sake of appearances.

She is still thinking like the proper princess she was in her father's kingdom, but this is not the way of the North. Our people do not do dangerous things for the sake of propriety and tradition. "You are not just any queen," I counter. "You are a queen of the North."

Her smile falters a moment, before she swallows hard and looks away.

It seems my words have upset her, but I do not understand why. I would ask for her thoughts, but I cannot do so here. I will have to wait until we are alone. It will not do to have my mate displeased with me.

CHAPTER 5

ANNA

He reminds me that I'm a queen of the North. His harsh tone suggesting that already, it seems, I'm a disappointment to him.

Tears sting my eyes, but I blink them back. I must find a way to make this work. I have to. He was right this morning to remind me that this marriage is to maintain the peace between our two kingdoms.

All my life I've been trained to be the perfect noblewoman. I've always tried my best to do what is expected of me. And yet, as I think of the disapproval in Henrick's tone, I realize that I am failing.

It's hard, but I somehow manage to keep the smile on my face until we've finally reached the edge of the city. As soon as we step out onto the open road, the mask slips from my face. My shoulders sag forward in exhaustion.

We travel in two rows with Henrick and me at the front. I turn back to see the long line of his men following us. Near the end of the line, Engrid gives me a small wave, and I return the gesture before facing ahead once again.

"We can send for the others once we arrive at Arnafell," Henrick says.

I'm surprised at this. "Why did we have to leave them behind, then?"

"As you pointed out, I am not a king without enemies." He's no doubt referring to the people of Ered. "We are vulnerable on the open road, and I did not want my men to worry about protecting anyone but you should we fall under attack."

I thought he was disappointed with me; I cannot deny my surprise at his high regard. Especially after I denied him my bed, and hinted I may deny him forever.

"Thank you," he murmurs.

"For what?"

"For doing all you could to convince your people that I am not their enemy. It was a wise move. It is obvious you are highly intelligent."

A bright smile lights my face at his compliment.

"Which is why I do not understand why you foolishly insist upon riding as you do," he adds.

My face falls as his praise turns to criticism.

Wounded pride gives way to anger. "Well, maybe *you* should have brought carriages for travel, like any *normal* king would do."

He stiffens. "I am not a normal king. I am the Bear King of the North, which means I was trained to think like a warrior. Carriages are not easily maneuverable. I did not want to risk you in such a cumbersome vessel. Especially when we travel over rougher terrain."

My anger dissipates instantly, leaving behind guilt in its wake. "Oh," I reply, unsure of what else to say now that I've insulted him, when he was only thinking of my safety.

He sighs heavily as we continue on. I hate that I spoke harshly to him. This isn't how I want things to be between us. I clear my throat. "I'm sorry. It's just... your manner of speaking is very blunt."

"I know," he replies.

I wait for him to continue. When he doesn't, I huff. "That's it? That is all you have to say after I apologized?"

"What else should I say?" he asks, confusion evident in his tone. "The way I speak—my bluntness, as you refer to it—is the way of the North. We speak only truth."

"I—" I stop abruptly, completely at a loss for words. In truth, I do not know how I expected him to answer. Maybe it's his gruff manners and his blunt way of speaking that trouble me.

But it seems this is something I will have to get used to.

I am married to this man and I'm searching for any hint of warmth or affection. But perhaps he is not capable of these things. I realize just how little I truly know about my new husband. I sigh. "I am... tired," I tell him, not wanting to speak of it further.

"Do you need to rest a moment?" he asks. "We could stop for a short break."

He may not be affectionate, but he is considerate of me, at least. And that is enough. For now. "No. We can continue on."

He dips his head in a subtle nod. "As you wish."

As the day wears on, the green plains begin to give way to rolling hills. I've heard Arnafell is a mountainous region covered by snow and ice. However, as we approach the border, I notice nothing but fields of farmland as far as the eye can see.

A village in the distance draws my attention. "Is that Islo?"

"Yes."

Relief floods me. I've heard of this quaint town but never

visited. I'm so tired, I'm glad our journey is almost done for the day.

"We will stop for an hour then continue on our way."

"What?" I blurt incredulously. "I thought we would stay here for the night."

He shakes his head. "We have made better time than I thought. It would be wiser to move on."

I open my mouth to protest but lose my nerve. Instead, I ask, "How much farther will we travel?"

"Until the sun has almost set."

I note the position of the sun in the sky. From what I can tell, it's at least three to four hours until sunset.

Perhaps resting for an hour will renew my strength.

Drawing closer to the village, we pass several homesteads along the outskirts. The houses appear to be all neat and well-kept. They are made of gray stone with thatched roofs. The cobbled streets appear clean and maintained. Despite how small the town appears, they do not seem to be wanting for anything.

People bow low in respect for their king and his men as we pass. Whether they do so out of loyalty or fear, I do not know, and that uncertainty has me on edge.

So far, Henrick seems to be somewhat agreeable, but I wonder just how long that will last.

When we reach the heart of the village, a crowd of people gathers in the square to greet their king. They wave banners with his sigil as children weave around Henrick's men, racing past the massive white bears seemingly without a fear or care in the world.

This is a good sign. His people are not afraid of the king's guards.

When we stop, one of the villagers approaches, dressed in long, gray robes. Judging by his rigid stance and the way the crowd parts for him, he's a man of importance—perhaps the

CLAIMED BY THE BEAR KING

town Elder, though I cannot be sure. He bows to Henrick and holds out folded clothing for him.

Henrick crouches, and I carefully slide off his back. No sooner do my feet touch the ground than I see him shift. He takes the robe from the man and wraps it around his nude form, covering himself.

"My King." The man bows again.

All the villagers drop to their knees, as well. Henrick takes my hand, lacing his fingers through mine. "This is my mate—Queen Anna of Arnafell, former princess of Ered."

The man blinks several times then bows a third time. He and the villagers raise their voices as one. "Long live King Henrick and Queen Anna."

Henrick turns to his men, and I notice several step forward, each carrying trunks. I wonder what they contain.

"I have brought food for the people," Henrick says, surprising me. "I understand much of your grain was taken during the raids."

"You are kind, my King. Thank you. We were not sure how to replenish our food stores."

Guilt and shame prick at my heart when I realize the raids must have been led by my father's men. After all, Islo is close to our kingdom's borders.

Henrick dips his chin and turns to me. "My queen and I will help distribute the food."

We are to help with the food? I'm shocked at his words. My mother and father would toss a few coins from time to time to the commoners, but never did they actively partici-pate in the distribution of goods to our people. It was beneath their station to do such a thing.

Or so, that is what my mother told me the one time I asked if I could help at the church, when I was younger.

"Thank you." The man smiles brightly. "You both honor us."

My muscles ache in protest from the full day's ride, but I force myself to ignore the pain as I follow Henrick's lead and help unload the food stores. Together, we deliver them into the waiting arms of his people.

My people, now.

With each item I hand out, the villagers greet me with warm smiles and sincere gratitude. Although I am tired, I find I do not mind doing this. In fact, I feel useful for the first time as far back as I can remember.

Back home, Mother always told me that my duty was to appear proper at all times. And once I was wed, it would be my job to please my husband in all things and to bear him as many heirs as was required to secure the throne.

As I observe Henrick, handing out food to the villagers, my heart melts a bit toward him. He is kind, my new husband. More so than I first believed. Perhaps I have made a sound decision after all.

He glances at me and I give him a faint smile.

Although he does not return it, I note the approval in his gaze before he turns back to his task, and my heart flutters in my chest.

Engrid walks up to me, leaning close as she whispers. "This is certainly a change, is it not?"

I know she refers to the few times we traveled with my father to the outlying towns of our kingdom. Instead of being greeted warmly, he was met with fear and anger. My father is the type of ruler who requires absolute fealty while doing very little to earn such devotion in return.

Engrid continues. "Your new husband is beloved by his people. This speaks very well of his character, does it not, my Lady?"

I nod as I glance once more at him, standing tall and proud, as he distributes goods to his people. When his eyes sweep to mine, with an approving gaze, warmth blooms across my cheeks in return.

She is right. Henrick may have a gruff demeanor, but he appears to be a kind man and a just ruler.

As I consider all of this, and study his handsome countenance, I am even more convinced I've made a sound decision in taking him as my husband.

CHAPTER 6

HENRICK

I t is easy to read the exhaustion in Anna's posture, yet she does not complain as she helps distribute food to our people.

A little girl runs up to her, tugging at her skirt. "Are you really the queen?"

Anna smiles as bright as the sun itself. She kneels until her face is level with the child. "Yes, I am, little one."

The child's eyes light with wonder. "You're beautiful."

"Why, thank you." Anna laughs softly, a light and cheery sound like the tinkling of bells or chimes. It's the first time I've heard it, and I'm already thinking of ways to coax another one from her lips.

I am surprised by Anna's expressiveness. Bear Shifters, we are a stoic lot, but I know that humans are not.

The little girl extends her arms, and Anna embraces her warmly in return. "Thank you for bringing us food. Mother was worried we might starve, but Father says we are saved now."

Anna's mouth drifts open as the little girl turns and skips back to her parents. When she stands, her eyes meet mine, bright with tears.

I frown as she approaches me and takes my hand. "You truly *are* a good king, aren't you?" she mutters only for my ears.

"The people needed food," I answer matter-of-factly. "What kind of ruler would allow his people to starve?"

A small line forms between her brows as she studies me, her eyes searching mine. For what? I do not know.

One of my men interrupts us. "My king, all the food has been distributed. We should continue on."

I turn to Anna, expecting her to protest that she is tired. Instead, she clenches her jaw and straightens her back as she prepares for more travel.

Shifting back into my bear form, I lower myself to the ground for Anna to climb onto my back. She hesitates for a moment, and when I turn to her, I watch her grab the hem of her skirt with both hands and pull it apart.

The material tears easily, leaving a slit up one side then the other so she does not have to ride side saddle on my back.

I push down a grin when she refuses to meet my gaze while clambering onto my back. She may be stubborn, but she is not foolish, it seems.

Once she is seated between my shoulders, one leg on either side, I call back to her, "Are you ready?"

Reluctantly, she nods. Despite her fatigue, she does not object. I wonder at this. Oryn, one of my guards, is mated to a human. I always thought of her as a fragile creature despite his insistence that she is not.

I thought traveling with Anna would prove difficult—that she would insist we stop for rest several times throughout the day—but she has ridden on my back without complaint. I doubted we'd reach Islo because of her. Not only have we made it, but we can go much farther. Our pace not slowed in the least to accommodate my queen or her lady-in-waiting.

Anna is stronger than I first thought, and this pleases me immensely.

We travel for a few more hours. As the sun sets, I halt at the base of the mountain pass.

"We're stopping?" Anna asks, and I note the hint of hope in her voice.

"Yes." I gesture to the mountains. "It is too dangerous to travel the pass at night. We will start early tomorrow."

Her eyes widen in study of the steep, winding trail before us. "We have to go up there?"

"Yes."

I pause, half-expecting her to argue it is not safe. Instead, she simply turns away and swallows thickly, trying to hide her obvious fear.

I call my bodyguard Aurick over.

"Yes, my King?"

"Guard the queen and her lady-in-waiting while I help set up the tents."

He dips his chin in a firm nod, and I start to leave, but Anna's small voice stops me. "Her name is Engrid."

I spin back and find her servant standing beside Anna, pale as a sheet. "Engrid." I repeat her name, committing it to memory. If this woman is important to Anna, I must remember her name. I glance at Aurick. "Stand guard over Queen Anna and Engrid."

"It would be my honor, my King."

I shift into my human form, as do the rest of my men. I notice Anna and Engrid's cheeks flushed deep red as they avert their eyes from me and my guards.

I walk over to Anna. "What is wrong?"

"You and your men... you're all naked."

33

I frown. "But you are my mate."

"Yes, but I am *your* mate, not *theirs*," she explains. "*You* are the only man I should ever see fully unclothed. And the only one to ever see me that way as well."

I knew that humans, in general, were uncomfortable with nudity, but I thought Anna would not care since she is my mate. Not wanting to distress her any further, I order my men to conjure the appearance of dark pants to hide their nakedness. I do the same.

It is taxing to keep up this illusion, but I do it for my mate. I want her to feel comfortable around me and my men.

While helping the men set up the tents, I lift my head to search for Anna, and to my surprise, I find her helping. Her long, chestnut hair is tied back in a loose knot at the nape of her neck. A few long tendrils have escaped, framing her lovely heart-shaped face.

Sensing my gaze upon her, she lifts her hazel eyes to mine and gives me a faint smile. Her cheeks are flushed from exertion, and her sleeves are rolled up to her elbows.

It seems she is not averse to hard work.

Perhaps, she will be a true queen of the North instead of the fragile flowers I thought humans to be. Princess Halla of Solwyck, whom I met not long ago, gave me pause, as well. Despite her broken body, she was not fragile either. Maybe I judge humans too harshly.

My guards must feel the same way. I observe them stealing glances at Anna, surprise and admiration in their faces. Their queen does not believe it beneath her to work alongside them.

This is good. A queen of the North should be humble. It seems the gods chose wisely for my fated one.

Once the tents are up, I make my way back to Anna's side. My nostrils flare, and I draw her scent deep into my lungs. It reminds me of roses and the fresh hint of spring. It is stronger after working so hard, and I clamp down on the need burning inside me in response to her enticing scent.

She purses her lips. "I know I smell bad. You don't have to be so obvious about it."

My head jerks back in shock. Does she believe I dislike her scent?

"What? That is not what—"

"Is there, by any chance, somewhere I can bathe? Or at least clean up?"

Oryn moves to my side, having overheard her request. "My King, I can escort the queen to the falls."

Even though he is already mated, a snarl pulls back my lips. After what Anna explained to me, I dislike the idea of any other male alone with my queen while she is unclothed. Her naked form is for my eyes only. Just as mine is only for hers. "I will take her." I turn back to Anna. "Come."

She follows me without hesitation, and I do not scent any fear from her.

This is progress. She knows I will not harm her; I am glad we are building trust. As soon as we reach the falls, I stop and face her expectantly.

Water cascades down the mountainside and into a large pool below. The crystalline surface reflecting the last of the sun's rays in a shimmering display of gold. A fine mist of steam rises from the water and Anna studies it curiously.

"It is heated." I answer her unspoken question. "A warm spring feeds into this waterfall."

She nods and then begins to unclasp the fasteners of her dress. Her cheeks flare bright red as I observe. "Can you... turn around?"

I frown. "Why?"

"Because I need to undress."

I blink slowly. She is my mate. Why would it be improper for me to see her unclothed? "We are married."

"Yes, but…" She hesitates a moment, her face flushed dark red. "We're still getting to know each other."

I move to reassure her. "If you are worried I will think you are ugly, your concern is unfounded. You are the most beautiful female I have ever seen."

Her mouth drifts open, and her cheeks turn an ever deeper shade of red. "I—I'm just a bit… embarrassed that's all," she says. "You're the first man to ever see me unclothed."

I frown. "Your previous lovers did not look upon you while mating?"

Her eyes widen, and she makes a strangled sound in the back of her throat. "I—I've never had any lovers. You will be my first. Why would you even think this of me?" she asks, obviously insulted.

My people mate for life, but I'd heard humans take many mates before they settle upon just one. Fierce possessiveness fills me at her words. I will be the first and only one that will ever join with her.

She blinks several times. "I cannot believe that you married me even though you thought I'd been with other men."

"Why would I not?" I answer, confused by her question.

"Because any other man would have insisted that I come to the marriage bed a virgin."

"I am not simply a man," I correct her. "I am a Bear Shifter. I'd heard that mating was a right of passage for your kind into adulthood, but it seems I was wrong. It would not have mattered to me if you'd taken any lovers before we met. All I ask is that you take no one else now that we are married."

"You are my *husband*, and the *only* man I will ever take to my bed, Henrick."

It's obvious that I have insulted her, but I have learned something even more important. Her answer indicates that she is not against the idea of joining with me after all. This is good. Now, I just have to wait for her to initiate our first mating. I am a patient male, but I cannot deny the hunger that burns inside me at the thought that someday she will accept me into her bed.

"Forgive me, Anna. I meant no insult."

She offers me a warm smile. "It's all right." She darts a glance back at the water. "Now, turn around."

"How am I supposed to guard you if I cannot see you?" I huff.

She purses her lips. "I promise I'll call out if I need you."

"Fine."

I turn my back and hear a soft rustle of fabric as she undresses. My stav hardens in response, but I grit my teeth, willing myself to calm.

I train my ears toward her, continually scanning the surrounding area for danger. A strange noise draws my attention, and I spin to find her standing under the falls.

Although I know I should avert my eyes, I find my body rooted in place, transfixed by her beautiful form. Her eyes are closed, the water cascading over her bare skin. My gaze travels over the sensuous mounds of her breasts, remembering their weight in my palm.

My mouth goes dry as the peaks stiffen and rivulets of water gather on the tips before falling. I allow my eyes to trail farther down her body, studying the slight dip of her waist and the gentle flare of her hips.

I force myself to turn away, knowing it will only displease her if she catches me staring at her nude form. I want her desperately, but I must wait until she invites me to her bed. I will not take her until she wants me.

If my dreams of her are truly visions of our future, I know it will eventually happen. She has haunted my sleep for many years.

The dream I cherish most is the one of her swollen with our child. She always stands on the balcony of our bedroom, staring out at the frozen sea. I approach and pull her into my arms, pressing a gentle kiss to her temple and splaying my hand over her abdomen. In my dreams, she turns in my arms and smiles up at me.

You are my mate, she whispers. *And I am yours.*

Even as the memory floats through my mind, I cannot fathom how it will come to pass.

My heart has been frozen since the blood witch cursed me. I cannot love. Not unless I find some way to melt the ice she placed around my heart.

CHAPTER 7

ANNA

W hen I am finished bathing, Henrick walks beneath the falls to wash off. As he strides toward the water, the illusion of his pants falls away, revealing a very muscular backside.

My cheeks flush with warmth as my gaze travels over his form. His entire body is thick planes of muscle; not an ounce of fat on him. He moves beneath the waterfall. Closing his eyes, he tips his head back as he allows the water to wash over him.

I know I should look away, but I cannot. My eyes move down his body and my cheeks flush with warmth.

He turns and his piercing blue eyes snap to mine as he catches me staring at him. I quickly lower my gaze, embarrassed that I've been caught.

He returns to my side, and I note that his pants are back on him again, thank goodness. His gaze is constantly sweeping the area around us, searching for any threat.

I don't want to ask what worries him, but I have to know. "What are you looking for?"

"Many predators make their homes both here and in the mountains."

"Nothing you and your guards can't handle, right?"

"Let us hope not."

His reply does nothing to assuage my fears, and now I feel foolish for insisting we leave the group to bathe. I walk close by his side as we make our way back to camp.

He wraps a possessive arm around my waist, tugging me against him. Something about his protectiveness makes my heart flutter in my chest. I cannot deny that he is a handsome man, and I love that he makes me feel safe and protected. It only adds to the attraction I am already feeling toward him.

As we approach the camp, I search the tents, trying to determine which one is his. Every time I traveled with my father, it was easy to spot the king's tent, much larger and more grandiose than the rest. But I do not notice any extravagant tents here.

I frown and turn to Henrick. "Where is your tent?"

He gestures to one near the middle, indistinguishable from the rest. "It is this one."

I glance around at the other tents. My mother's was slightly smaller than my father's, and easy to spot. But I cannot tell which one is meant for me. "Which one is mine?"

His piercing eyes meet mine as he gestures to his tent. "This one."

I'm surprised he wants me to stay with him. My father always slept apart from my mother, both at home and anytime we traveled. I asked my mother about this once, and she said they had an understanding. She had already given him two heirs. After that, my father felt no further need for them to share a bed.

Part of me wonders if Henrick will be like my father. I

hope not, but I cannot be sure. There might never be love between us; it is too soon to tell. But I pray there can, at least, be mutual respect and understanding. I do not know how my mother endured the shame of having the entire kingdom know her husband had bedded nearly every woman in the royal court.

I follow Henrick inside the tent. In the center, a small fire flickers, the smoke escaping through a hole in the ceiling of the cloth cover. Close by lies a large bedroll. I swallow thickly when I note there is only one.

I stand undecided, glancing at Henrick and wondering what he expects. He said he would not touch me until I asked, but perhaps he has changed his mind.

As if reading my thoughts, he turns to me. "I already told you: We will not mate against your will."

My cheeks flush as he loses the illusion of his pants, and stands naked before me. I swallow hard and cast a tentative look down his body to his length. He's much larger than I thought a man would be, even when he is not aroused. Then again, he is not a man. He is a Bear Shifter, as he pointed out.

"I apologize if my nudity makes you uncomfortable," he says. "It is taxing to keep the illusion of clothing for long periods of time."

I like that he cares what I think, but I'm curious to understand if clothing is optional among his people at all times. "Do your people often walk around unclothed?"

"It is not uncommon while we are traveling."

"Why is that?"

"Out in the open, we prefer to be prepared to shift whenever necessary to defend ourselves." He cocks his head to the side. "We are mated. Does my nudity truly bother you?"

"I—" I'm not sure what to say. "It's just… as I've said, you are the first man I've ever seen naked. My people do not normally walk around uncovered."

"It will not be this way once we reach the castle. Come to bed," he murmurs, his voice low and deep. "I will keep you warm this night."

I gulp against the knot of nervousness in my stomach and slowly move to his side. I'm not averse to sharing a bed with him; I'm just not sure I'm ready to share what a wife does with her husband.

He sits on the bedroll, tugging me down with him. Then he throws his arms around me and pulls me against his chest. He drags the blanket over us and curls his body protectively around mine.

Henrick's masculine scent—like fresh rain and forest—fills my nostrils. Warmth floods my body as I draw in a deep breath. He tightens his arms around my waist, and his breath is warm against the back of my neck.

"You have done better than I expected," he mutters in my ear.

I turn my head back to face him. "How so?"

"Humans are weak. I doubted we'd make it this far so quickly."

I bristle at his comment. "Just because I cannot shift into a bear does not mean I'm weak."

A soft chuckle escapes him. "*There* is your fire."

"What?"

"I was not sure you had it when we were first wed. I have only seen glimpses of it on our travels, but I see it clearly now."

I frown. "You want me to argue with you?"

"No. I simply wish to hear your truth. That is all."

"My truth? What are you talking about?"

"I want you to speak your mind."

"*Now* you want me to speak my mind?" I ask incredulously. "After you demanded my hand in marriage to keep peace between our kingdoms?"

His head jerks back. "I asked if you agreed to marry me of your own free will, and you said *yes*."

I blink at the cloth wall. "How was I supposed to deny you? You defeated my father in battle. You would have taken away our kingdom and—"

"Why would you assume this?" he interjects.

I scoff. "That's what conquerors do. They take what they want." I pause, wondering whether I should continue. "Why do you think my father offered me to you? I paid his price so he may keep his lands and title."

A muted but fierce sound rumbles his chest. The hair rises on the back of my neck as his eyes flash with anger. "I did not ask for such payment. Your father suggested the marriage when I told him I was in search of a mate. He told me you agreed to this. I made *no* demands."

"What did you expect him to do?" I ask incredulously. "Deny your request?"

"I would have expected *you* to deny it if you did not want me."

"How could I deny you?" I counter. "I was afraid."

He looks at me as if struck. "And now?"

"I—I don't know," I answer honestly. "Part of me is still worried… afraid to make you upset. That you might snap or—"

"I would never harm a female." His voice deepens. "It is dishonorable. And my people speak only truth; it is the way of the North. As their queen, you'd do well to remember this."

Without warning, he stands and moves to the door of the tent. I jerk upright. "Where are you—"

Before I can finish, he's already gone.

CHAPTER 8

HENRICK

As soon as I leave the tent, I shift forms, running along the perimeter, trying to burn off the anger roiling inside me.

She did not want me. She lied when I asked her if she had agreed to the marriage.

Our bonding began with a lie. She is afraid of me—so much so that she withheld the truth. Now, she is bound to me against her will.

I am a fool.

I thought she was simply nervous about our joining. I did not realize she was completely averse to me.

Circling the encampment, I pass several of my men standing guard who are probably wondering why I left my mate—the female who wants nothing to do with me.

I cannot keep her. Nor will I force her to stay with me.

When I first saw her, I believed it was destiny that we had found one another. I'd agreed to the marriage her father proposed because I needed a mate. When I stepped into the forest and saw her standing under the winter's moon, I believed the gods were smiling down upon me, giving me their blessing by presenting the very woman I had been dreaming of for so long.

I thought it was a sign—an end to my curse. I thought she was the one who could melt the ice the Snow Queen placed around my heart. But it seems I was wrong.

Making my way back to the tents, I shift into my human form and gather several furs from the provisions trunk for Anna.

Bitter acid rises in my throat at the thought of how terrified she probably was. And I hate that she fears me even now, when I have done nothing but try to protect her and keep her safe.

Even as I think this, guilt fills me. I left her just now. In the cold, with only a blanket and a low fire to warm her. I am a terrible mate to my new bride. She is not only afraid of me... I have been negligent in my care of her.

I tuck the furs under my arms and head back to our tent.

I may be unable to love, but I am not a monster.

The morning after our wedding night, I thought she was worried that I would reject her because she did not share my bed. I did not realize she was hoping that I would leave her behind and annul our marriage.

With a heavy sigh, I shake my head. I hate that she feels trapped and afraid. That is the last thing I would ever want her to feel. I will release her from her vows; I will not keep Anna against her wishes. If she wants to return to her family, I will see it done.

When I enter the tent, she is asleep near the fire. Her body shivers, and I'm overcome with guilt. Despite my anger, I should not have left her. She is human and cannot regulate her body temperature nearly as effectively as my people can.

Carefully, I drape the furs over her, tucking them around

her shoulders for added insulation. I shift back into my bear form and lie down beside her. To my surprise, she instinctively curls into my side for warmth.

Fierce protectiveness fills me as she nestles against me.

I hate that she believes she had no choice but to marry me. I will not try to coerce her to remain at my side if it is not her desire.

I stare down at her smaller form, and gently drape my arm over her body, careful to make sure my weight does not crush her.

As I study her delicate features, I am once more overcome by the knowledge that she is just as I have dreamed. The gods gave me those visions of her for a reason. Or so I believed.

I was given a gift—a blessing that many hope for, but never find.

Perhaps this is part of the curse. Everything I touch turns to bitter ash.

Anna sighs softly and snuggles even closer. Already, I had begun to think of her as mine. Although I had not claimed her, I still considered her my mate. My queen. But now I see that I have failed her miserably.

Once more, I am in awe of her strength. Even despite her fear, she still married me, stood up to me, and then was brave enough to tell me the truth I had asked for.

A heavy sigh escapes me. I will not keep her against her will. I vow to do everything I can to make this right for her.

My gaze travels over her once more. Long lashes fan over soft pink cheeks and her lips are parted in a small o. As I study her, a thought begins to form: What if I could convince her to stay?

As I stare up at the stars, the idea begins to take hold. It is a long journey to Arnafell. The time between here and there can be spent convincing her that I am worthy to be her mate. I cannot stand the thought of losing her. Not now that I know the female I have always dreamed of is real.

There must be a reason the gods made our paths to cross. She is my Fated One. Of this, I am certain. I will do everything I can to please her. And perhaps by the time we reach Arnafell, she will wish to stay and be mine.

CHAPTER 9

ANNA

The first thing I become aware of is that I'm completely surrounded by warmth. My eyes snap open to find Henrick asleep beside me in his human form. I'm snug under a layer of furs and tucked into his side. I appreciate that, despite his anger, he cared enough to come back and keep me warm.

He's still asleep, so I take a moment to observe him. He was genuinely upset at the idea that I married him because I thought he had demanded it of my father. His anger speaks volumes; he's not a terrible man who would demand a tribute simply because he can. And he Is not a bloodthirsty warrior like I'd heard.

I realize now that if I'd told him I did not want to go through with our marriage, he would not have pushed me nor threatened to take away my father's lands or title. He simply wanted a mate and the alliance our marriage could forge.

Henrick is a warrior, but he does not like the idea of war.

That much was evident when he made sure the people of Islo were fed after suffering through border skirmishes with my father's guards.

His eyelids open, and his ice-blue eyes find mine.

"Thank you," I whisper.

His brow furrows. "For what?"

"Coming back even though you were upset."

"I should not have left you to the cold."

I attempt a faint smile. "You didn't. You came back."

"There is something we must discuss," he says, and something about his tone fills me with dread.

"What is it?"

He grimaces. "You need not fear me, Anna. I would never harm you. I am your mate, but you have my vow, I will not touch you until you ask."

"And what if I never do?" The question escapes my lips before I can catch it, but I will not take it back. Besides, I have already told him this before. I have to know he means what he says. "What if I do not want to share a bed with you in any manner—even just to sleep?"

"Then so be it," he answers, just as he did at the castle on our wedding night. He stands and turns to leave.

"Where are you going?"

"To guard," he replies, not bothering to turn back.

I lay my head down, allowing my exhaustion to take over. I watch him shift back into his bear form and lie down just inside the entrance.

My lips part on a breath at the realization he is guarding our tent. The dim light of the fire casts an orange glow across his thick, white fur. I watch his breaths become deep and even.

Flakes of snow drift down from the hole in the tent, disappearing almost as soon as they appear in the light of the flame.

With a heavy sigh, I consider my situation. I'm married to a man who has vowed not to touch me until I ask. He's kinder and more thoughtful than I ever expected. Perhaps there is no love between us now, but if he is truly as kind as he seems, maybe it will follow.

Closing my eyes, I turn over in bed, my head spinning with possibilities as I realize this isn't the dreadful existence I feared it would be.

CHAPTER 10

HENRICK

When I wake in the morning, Anna is still asleep. I shift forms, making sure to conjure the image of pants to cover me from the waist down for her sake. I've instructed my men to continue doing the same. I do not want to make her uncomfortable.

Kneeling beside her, I study her face as she sleeps. Her long, chestnut hair is spread out beneath her like a beautiful halo. She is even lovelier than she was in my dreams.

When I reach down and tenderly brush the hair back from her face, her eyelids flutter open. As soon as her hazel eyes find mine, she jerks upright. "What time is it? Did I sleep for too long?"

A smile quirks my lips. "No, you did not."

"Then what—"

"I was simply checking on you."

Her gaze drops to the blankets and furs over her. "Thank you, Henrick. It was cold last night, but these helped."

I dip my chin in a subtle acknowledgment. "You are my queen. It is my duty to tend to you."

She blinks several times. "Tend to me?"

"Yes. You are my mate. It is my desire that you are comfortable and your needs provided for."

She blinks several times as she regards me.

"Is this not the human way?" I ask, curious to understand her expression.

She lowers her gaze. "With my parents, it was my mother who had to make sure my father was... pleased at all times. It's how I was raised and what I was told would be expected of me by my husband someday."

What sort of male expects his mate to care for his needs and think nothing of hers in return? Placing two fingers up under her chin, I tip her face back up to mine. "In my culture, females are treasured. Their mates tend to their needs and see to their comfort and protection. Always."

A faint smile crests her lips. "That sounds lovely."

"Anna, I—"

Aurick steps into our tent, interrupting. "My King. My Queen." He bows low. "We have already begun breaking down the camp."

It occurs to me that he is entirely too informal with me—his king—sometimes, but I cannot fault him for it. Aurick and I grew up together. We were friends before he became my most trusted guard.

"Good," I reply, turning to Anna to gently urge her to get ready as quickly as possible. She doesn't give me the chance, rolling up the bedding without complaint.

It doesn't take her long to dress, and a smile quirks my lips when I notice she has torn a line on either side of her skirt, ready to travel comfortably again today. Practical and efficient. Like a true queen of the North.

After packing, my guards and I shift forms. I crouch, and

Anna climbs easily onto my back, settling over my shoulders.

"Did you eat?"

She reaches into her pocket and pulls out two strips of dried meat. She flashes a grin. "I came prepared for travel."

I dip my chin. "Good thinking, my Queen."

Her cheeks flush deep red.

I turn and start for the mountains. When we draw closer, I feel her muscles tense, so I stop. "What is wrong?"

"How are we going to cross the mountains?"

"There is a passage we use. The one I showed you yesterday." I gesture with my snout. "Do you see that trail up the wall?"

A soft gasp escapes her, and I turn my head to look back. Her eyes are wide.

"We're going up that incline?"

"Yes," I reply calmly. "My people take this passage often."

I wait for her to say something else, but she snaps her jaw shut. I continue toward the mountain, and as soon as we reach the base, I stop again. "The passage is very steep. You must hold tightly to me. Do you think you can do this?"

Her small brow furrows, but she does not protest. Instead, she draws in a deep breath and gives me a determined nod. "Yes."

As I start up the incline, the acrid scent of her fear fills my nostrils. I wrinkle my nose against the terrible smell and wish there were some way to comfort her. But I cannot stop, nor can I look back. I must concentrate on my footing.

She does not make a sound. Her hands and legs grip me tightly as she lies almost completely flush against my back. Her heart beats wildly in her chest.

She is much braver than I realized.

"Are you all right?" I ask over my shoulder.

"Yes," she replies in an even voice, and I cannot help but admire her at this moment, for she hides her fear very well.

CHAPTER 11

ANNA

As Henrick ascends the steep incline in his bear form, I'm surprised by his fast, agile gait. Cold wind whips around us, clawing at my form, but I hold tight to him. We travel for an hour or so, though it feels like forever. I make the mistake of glancing back to gauge our progress and immediately become dizzy.

I lean forward, sinking my hands into his thick fur. "Please don't let me fall," I whisper under my breath.

"Never. I will keep you safe, Anna."

Closing my eyes, I lie flat against him, holding on for dear life. My heart hammers, and I struggle to focus on my breathing, drawing in several slow and steadying breaths that bring me his scent of fresh rain and forest. It's comforting somehow, and I close my eyes, concentrating on the way he moves beneath me.

The muscles of his form are strong. Each flex of his back and legs speaks of strength and power. Yet he is gentle with me, even though he does not have to be. He could have forced himself upon me on our wedding night and demanded I surrender because we are married. But he didn't; he hasn't.

I realize the mountainside would have been much easier for him to scale without a rider on his back. He could have passed me off to one of his men, but he did not. Even after I told him I may never invite him to my bed, he still cares enough to carry me himself.

"We have almost reached a plateau where you can rest."

A heavy sigh of relief escapes my lungs. "Thank goodness."

By the time the ground evens, every muscle in my body is aching and sore from clinging to Henrick during the steep climb.

He stops, and I slide off his back. As soon as my feet hit the ground, my legs give out from under me, and I stumble forward.

Henrick immediately shifts forms and catches me around the waist, lifting me into his arms. Gently, he brushes the hair back from my face, his ice-blue eyes studying me in concern. "Are you all right?"

It's on the tip of my tongue to lie and insist that I am fine, but he said he only wants truth. So, instead, I reply. "I'm tired."

I glance back to look for Engrid and see the rest of Henrick's guards still making their way up the pass.

I didn't realize we were so far ahead of everyone.

He peers at the sky, searching for potential threats. "You must eat and drink something to keep up your strength. We have much farther to go. We will not be safe until we are on the other side of the mountain."

A frisson of fear moves through me at his suggestion that we might be in danger, from something other than potentially falling to our deaths. "What are you worried about? Is there something up here that could harm us?"

He dips his chin in a subtle nod. "Griffins sometimes make their homes in the mountains."

I swallow against the sudden knot of worry churning my stomach. "Griffins?"

"Yes."

Although I've never seen one, I have heard tales. Griffins are dangerous, deadly creatures nearly impossible to kill. With the body and tail of an enormous lion and the head and wings of an eagle, they are fearsome creatures to behold.

Their razor-sharp talons are their most lethal feature. They can tear a man to shreds in an instant.

Henrick hands me a waterskin and some more dried meat since I already ate the rations I kept in my pockets earlier.

I sit with my back against a rock wall, and he sinks to the ground beside me, his gaze constantly scanning the area around us for danger.

"Have you ever seen a Griffin before?" I ask, already dreading his answer.

"Yes."

I wait a moment for him to elaborate. When he does not, I push. "Well?"

He turns to me. "Well, what?"

"What happened?"

"Many of my men were injured, and a few died."

"How many Griffins were there?"

"Only one," he replies. "We were fortunate."

If that's what he considers fortunate, I cannot imagine what a disaster would be like. "Fortunate?" I ask incredulously. "But you lost some of your men."

He nods. "Aye, but it could have been worse."

I dart a glance at our surroundings with renewed fear.

"Why did we come this way if there might be Griffins? Why not take the main road between the mountains?"

He turns to me as if my question were strange. "You would rather have potentially faced Wraiths?"

"Wraiths?"

"Yes. The forest is full of them. The winter winds are already here, promising snow soon. I did not want to risk being trapped in the forest at nightfall if we encountered bad weather. Wraiths prefer the taste of human flesh to all others. They are known to hunt in packs, whereas Griffins do not. Given the choice, I believed it would be easier to keep you safe from one predator instead of several."

I suppose he's right. If I had to choose between Wraiths or Griffins, I'd have chosen the same as him.

I swallow hard as he returns his focus to the sky. Fear coils around my chest, and I send a silent prayer to whoever may be listening that we do not encounter any Griffins.

My gaze travels up the mountain pass, stretching high above us and disappearing into the clouds. I'm terrified by the mere sight, wondering if death awaits us up there.

"Are you well, my Queen?" Engrid's voice rips me from my thoughts.

I lift my gaze to her and smile brightly, happy to see her.

Aurick, Henrick's personal guard, walks up behind her. It doesn't escape my notice how her cheeks flush as soon as she sees him.

Henrick goes to speak with Aurick and the rest of their men while Engrid takes a seat beside me. My eyes track my husband as he leaves. "I do not quite understand him," I murmur.

"You are only newly wed, my Lady. It will take time for you to learn about each other."

"All the stories I heard of him... he was described as a terrifying monster. And yet, he is kind to me. Gentle even." I sigh heavily. "Part of me worries that he will lose patience with me, and become the terrible man Father made him out to be."

Engrid takes my hand, her green eyes searching mine in concern. "Why are worried he will lose patience with you?"

I flick my gaze back to Henrick, observing him in the distance, talking to his men. "Because I have not taken him to my bed yet," I admit. "He told me that he will not touch me until I ask him to."

Engrid gives me a warm smile and squeezes my hand. "This is a good sign, my Lady. It means you have married well. Any man who would say this is honorable indeed."

She gestures to Aurick. "Your husband's men speak very highly of him. They say he is a fair and just King. I believe you have made a good choice in marrying him."

"He seems a bit... cold though, does he not?" I ask. "His manner of speaking is often very blunt."

"I believe this may just be their way," Engrid says. "I asked Aurick about this and he says it is the 'way of the North.'"

I think back on my conversation with Henrick when he told me he only wanted me to always speak truthfully to him. Perhaps, his blunt speech is simply an expression of this.

As if somehow knowing that I'm talking about him, Henrick's head snaps to mine.

I flash a smile at him and his lips quirk up slightly at the edges as he returns it with one of his own. He truly is a handsome man. I imagine a full smile on his face would be devastatingly gorgeous.

"You are blushing, my Lady," Engrid teases gently.

I playfully bump her shoulder with mine, and arch a brow. "I saw you do the same with Aurick."

She laughs. "I cannot help it. He's very handsome and kind. And he is so thoughtful and protective as well." Her expression sobers as she lifts her gaze to the sky. "He warned me that there might be Griffins here."

I nod. "Henrick told me the same."

As if my very thoughts have summoned him, Henrick strides over to us. He extends his hand. I take it, and he pulls me up to his side.

Engrid excuses herself and returns to Aurick.

Henrick holds out a blade. "I retrieved this from our supplies. I want you to keep it on you at all times."

He tucks the knife into my belt and then carefully folds my cloak around me a bit tighter to make sure I'm protected from the cold wind. This extra care he takes with me warms my heart. "Thank you."

"Of course," he replies, his voice deep and smooth like velvet. "Are you ready to continue, or do you wish to rest a bit more?"

His consideration makes me smile. "I am ready."

CHAPTER 12

ANNA

Henrick shifts into bear form again and kneels for me to climb onto his back. As I'm about to ascend, a large shadow blocks the sun, and a shrill cry pierces the air. My head whips toward the sky, and I stare, frozen in fear, as a Griffin weaves through the clouds.

"Take shelter!" one of the men yells as the Griffin circles overhead.

My pulse pounds in my ears as its gaze locks onto mine, like a predator sizing up its prey.

It releases another angry cry before it folds its wings to its back, and dives straight for us.

"Get down!" Henrick shouts.

Lightning fast, he pushes me to the ground, covering me with his massive form.

A loud *thud* sounds above as the Griffin slams into his back. Henrick releases a bellowing roar as he tumbles away from me, swiping out with his massive paws and catching the Griffin's side.

It releases a deafening cry as Henrick's sharp claws rake across its body, drawing blood.

The pull away from each other, and Henrick positions himself directly between me and the Griffin. He bares his fangs as a deep growl rumbles in his chest.

The Griffin's large talons scrape the ground as it stalks toward him, craning its neck to look around him, to me.

"Human flesh," the Griffin hisses, voice low and threatening. "Let me have her, and I'll allow you to pass. It has been a long time since I have tasted tender meat. Give her to me."

"No," Henrick snarls. "You cannot have her."

"Then you will die."

Without warning, he rushes toward Henrick. They clash in a blur of claws and fangs then roll in a tangled mess of limbs. Aurick and two of the other guards rush to the king's defense, joining the fray.

Henrick releases a thunderous roar as the Griffin drags its claws across his chest. Dodging too late, Henrick and his men circle the Griffin, crimson blood dripping on the ground all around them.

With a flap of its wings, it lifts into the air and swoops toward me. My pulse pounds in my ears as time slows. I twist my body, trying to spin away, but I'm not fast enough.

The world shifts into slow motion as sharp talons wrap around my waist. I cry out as they dig deep into my side.

"Anna!" Henrick rushes toward me, and I reach for him, but he's too far away.

His eyes meet mine full of unbridled panic as the Griffin flaps his enormous wings, lifting into the air in a rush of wind.

"Henrick!"

A terrified cry erupts from my throat as I'm ripped away into the sky.

The vise-like grip around my waist squeezes the air from my lungs, abruptly cutting off my scream as we ascend above the clouds. I watch in horror as the world falls away beneath me, and my husband releases an angry roar. His bellow of rage echoing over the mountainside.

Desperate to escape, I struggle against the Griffin's hold, but it's no use. He responds by tightening his grasp, making it painful to breathe. Unable to free my blade from my belt, I claw and bite at him, but his hide is too thick to do any damage.

My heart hammers as we continue to climb. I have to find a way to free myself. Fear threatens to overwhelm me, but I force myself to push it back down. The pain in my sides is nearly unbearable, but I bite my bottom lip, struggling to hold in my tears.

I have to focus. If I allow myself to give in to panic, I'll die for sure. I have to keep my wits about me.

After what feels like an eternity, the Griffin dips his left wing and begins to circle a rocky ledge near the peak of the mountain. As we draw closer, I notice a large pile of branches and leaves stacked neatly beneath an overhang.

He drops me down into the strange formation; the force of the impact lessened as I land on a thick layer of grass. I wince at the pain in my sides as I force myself to stand on unsteady legs. My heart stops when I notice three large eggs nearby.

They are each half a head taller than me and at least three times as wide.

This is a nest, and I am to be their meal.

My pain is quickly forgotten as the Griffin cocks his head to the side. "Do not try to escape, human," he says darkly. "I will only find you again."

Before I can respond, he flies away.

Full blown panic sets in. I move as far from the eggs as I can and begin climbing up the side. It's so tall and steep I don't even make it half way up before I lose my footing, and go tumbling back onto the thick grass lining the bottom of the nest.

Fear spikes through me. "Help! Someone, please!"

I'm not sure whom I expect to hear me. We flew so high, I doubt anyone will find me in time.

A cold wind whips around my form, chilling me to the bone. I grip the knife at my belt, but I worry it will not be enough to save me. Not from monsters like these.

My thoughts turn to Henrick, and I wonder if he will even bother to search for me. After all, we're newly married, and I refused his advances.

I denied him my bed and my affections. I suggested we annul our marriage before we left my father's kingdom. Now that I'm missing, what reason would he have to search for me? I've practically told him I might never give in and provide him with heirs.

What use does a king have for a queen who refuses him?

Alone with only my fears and dark thoughts to keep me company, I keep searching for any way to climb out of the nest, but it's no use. Still, I try. To admit defeat would only lead to despair, and I'm not ready to give up just yet.

A sharp *crack* fills the air, and dread overwhelms me. This sound can mean only one thing. Slowly, I spin to face the eggs. Fine fissures form, crackling as they spread out along the shells. The baby Griffins are about to hatch, and as soon as they do, I'm dead.

I pull the knife from my belt and hold it out before me as I face the eggs. Whatever happens, I will not go gently to my death.

A dark shadow falls over me, and I turn to see not one,

but two Griffins above me, each with narrowed, predatory eyes.

Ice floods my veins as my gaze drops to their large and deadly talons, curled over the edge of the nest.

"You would harm my fledglings?" the mother hisses, gripping the wood so tight it begins to give beneath her.

"Drop the blade," her mate snarls.

Despite my trembling, I grit my teeth and move closer to the nearest egg. "No!"

The only thing keeping the parents from attacking me is their concern that I might harm one of the eggs with my knife. I know if I lose my weapon, I'm dead. Though as I eye the two adult Griffins on the edge of the nest, I'm not sure anything can save me now.

A deafening roar splits the air, stopping my heart.

The Griffins spin toward the sound.

Out of the corner of my eye, I notice a flash of white fur. I recognize Henrick immediately as he slams into the male. They crash into the nest in a clash of fur, fangs, and claws. Henrick's bear form is slightly larger than the Griffin, but there are two of them. He is outnumbered and I worry he'll be easily outmatched.

The female rushes to defend her mate. With her back to me, I take advantage of her distraction and charge. Using every bit of my strength, I sink my blade deep into her flesh.

It cuts through her hide with a sickening squelch, and she stumbles back.

I pull the knife free, and she spins toward me, rage burning in her eyes. "You will die, you pitiful human."

She charges me, but Henrick's massive paw swipes out, catching her side. She slams against the nest and falls still.

He returns his attention to the male, and they begin circling one another. Blood drips from Henrick's back and sides onto the thick grass below.

The Griffin rushes, sinking his talons deep into Henrick's flesh and lifting him into the air. Henrick twists in his grasp, swiping with his claws, and they go tumbling back to the ground, just outside the nest.

Through the small gaps in the nesting materials, I watch as they rip and tear at each other, locked in a deadly embrace.

My heart pounds as Henrick fights the Griffin. I'm desperate to reach him; to help him somehow.

Glancing at the still form of the female, an idea forms. I climb up her body, pulling myself the rest of the way to the top of the nest.

My eyes widen as I look over the side, to the ground below. It's a long drop, but I don't have a choice. I have to reach Henrick. I need to help him.

I grip the ledge firmly, and lower myself as far as I can. Hanging for a moment on the edge, I steel myself and then release my grasp, falling to the ground below.

The sharp pain in my sides steals the breath from my lungs, but I force myself to stand. Gripping the blade tightly in my hand, I barrel toward the Griffin.

He twists at the last moment and my blade misses its intended mark. Instead of cutting his back, I tear a line down his wing.

It isn't much of a distraction, but that's all Henrick needs. He lunges forward, raking his sharp claws across the male's neck and slicing deep.

Blood gushes from the Griffin's wound, his eyes wide as choked, gurgling sounds escape his throat. He collapses in a pool of blood.

Henrick turns to me. "Quickly! Climb onto my back! We must leave in case there are more of them nearby!"

I do as he asks without hesitation. His white fur is dark and sticky with his blood, but I manage to cling to him as he rushes away. He clambers off the peak then picks a narrow

CLAIMED BY THE BEAR KING

path winding around the mountain. I have to squeeze my eyes shut for fear I'll lose the contents of my stomach if I peer over the edge.

The wounds on my torso, from the Griffin's talons, have become a dull, aching throb. It's painful, but not unbearably so. I'm more concerned about Henrick. His wounds are many and seeping blood on his normally white coat.

"Are your guards nearby?" I ask, praying he says yes. I'm not sure how much further he'll be able to travel with his injuries.

"Yes. We agreed upon a meeting place before we left in search of you. They should still be there," he adds. "But we will not reach them tonight. I must find a place to recover and rest."

I open my mouth, ready to insist that I walk instead of ride on his back, but he interrupts. "The mountain pass is too steep for you to safely traverse. I may be injured, but is not a burden to carry you, Anna."

I would argue, but he's right. If I were to walk, there is a high probability I might lose my footing and fall to my death.

After what feels like an eternity, we reach a plateau with a small cavern. Henrick walks inside then collapses to the stone floor in a crumpled heap.

"Henrick!"

He shifts into his two-legged form, naked on the ground beside me. I lift his head into my lap and cup his cheek, turning his face to me.

His eyes open, and he blinks up at me. "Are you all right?" he groans.

"Am *I* all right?" I ask incredulously, surveying his bloodied, injured form. Deep gashes from the Griffin's claws span the length of his chest, blood seeping from the wounds and pooling around him. "You're the one who's hurt."

"I will heal. I just need time."

The echo of water falling nearby captures my attention, and I notice a small pool near the back of the cavern. I carefully place his head on the ground and get to my feet. "There's water here. I need to clean your wounds."

Without waiting for him to reply, I make my way to the back of the cave. The sun is still up, lighting my way so I do not stumble.

I find two pools. Dropping to my knees, I feel the ground is warm beneath me and dip my hands into the water to discover it's pleasantly hot.

The larger pool is fed by a smaller one beside it, which sits slightly higher. Cupping a handful of water to taste it, I note no bitterness in the flavor.

We should be able to drink from the first one and bathe in the second.

I roll up my sleeves to my elbows, tying my hair back into a loose knot at the nape of my neck before ripping a few strips from my dress and plunging them into the water. Quickly, I return to Henrick's side.

His eyes search mine. "What are you—"

"I'm going to clean you up. This might sting a little."

The moment I touch the cloth to his skin, he hisses through his teeth but remains impressively still.

He grips my forearm, his gaze dropping to the wounds on my torso and the blood staining my dress. "What about you?"

"My injuries are not deep like yours. I'll be fine."

"I should be the one caring for you," he rasps. "It is my responsibility to—"

I press a finger to his lips to silence him. "Shush. Just be still. You must conserve your strength."

Before he can argue, I leave to return to the pool. I go back and forth between him and the pool several times, cleaning his wounds and his body.

When I'm finished, I'm exhausted and cold. The sun is

nearly gone. As night settles in, it carries a cool wind that whips through the cavern, making me shiver.

I take Henrick's hand. "Do you think you can move closer to the back of the cave? It is warmer back there."

"Yes."

I do my best to help him to his feet, but he's so heavy that I'm not sure how much support I can provide. Still, I wrap his arm around my shoulders, and together we hobble toward the warm springs.

As soon as we reach a clear spot, he practically collapses again. I drop to my knees beside him. "What do you need? Tell me."

A heavy sigh escapes him. "I will heal. I just need time."

"How long?"

His brow furrows. "A day. Maybe a bit more."

"All right."

I glance down at my clothes, sticky and covered in blood. Normally, I'd be too embarrassed to undress in front of him, but at this moment, I find I do not care.

"I'm going to bathe and wash my clothes."

Grabbing the hem of my dress, I lift the garment over my body, stopping short when I feel his hand alight on my torso. I discard my dress to the side as he runs his fingers near the puncture wounds on my skin, his eyes tracing over the brutal red marks. They are not as deep as I thought but they are painful, nonetheless.

His worried gaze meets mine. "You are injured, Anna."

"I'll be fine."

A frown mars his face as he places two fingers under my chin and tips my face up. His ice-blue eyes are disapproving. "You should not have attacked the Griffin."

"I was trying to help you," I huff. "I was afraid he would kill you."

His frown deepens. "My kind are not so easily killed."

I place my hands on my hips. "But no one is invincible, Henrick."

His eyes lock onto mine a moment before he turns his attention to the cave's entrance. "Darkness is upon us. We will rest here tonight and continue in the morning."

"Are you sure you'll be well enough to travel by then? I could go search for the others... bring back help."

"I am not weak," he grumbles.

"I didn't say you were weak."

"You did not have to," he mutters. "It was implied."

"I won't argue with you. If you're well enough in the morning, we'll leave together. If you are not, I will search for the others and bring them back here."

"You will not leave without me," he growls. "You could be hurt—"

"Don't you growl at me!" I snap. "You need to focus on saving your strength and getting better."

Gritting his teeth, he lifts his eyes to the cave's ceiling, but remains silent.

Satisfied, I turn toward the warm springs. A soft hiss escapes me when I slip beneath the warm water, but my skin only stings for a moment before the pain dissipates. When I'm finished washing the blood from my skin, I step out of the water then rinse my clothes and place them on a nearby rock to dry.

Henrick's stare is heavy on me as I return to his side, kneeling beside him to examine his wounds. The move farther into the cave caused some of his injuries to begin bleeding again.

"I should clean these again."

"You should rest, Anna. You are injured as well. I will heal shortly and—"

"*Henrick,*" I practically growl. "I'm going to take care of you, whether you like it or not."

His lips form a tight, thin line, but he does not argue.

CHAPTER 13

HENRICK

Fire blazes across my skin when she cleanses my wounds. I was exhausted before, so it was easier to hold my tongue while she tended to me. But now that I am more alert, my wounds sting, and I bite back a snarl as she drags the cloth across the gaping marks the Griffin scored into my chest.

The fact that she cares enough to tend my injuries pleases me immensely. But it is so painful, I would rather she leave them be.

I grip her wrist firmly just before it touches my skin. Her eyes snap up, and I grit my teeth. "You do not need to do this. I already told you, I will heal, Anna."

She sticks out her chin. "I'm trying to help you." Her gaze holds mine intently, unwilling to back down. "It will only sting for a moment."

I release my grasp. "Fine," I murmur, narrowing my eyes. "But it is much more than a mere *sting*. Your ministrations hurt more than the initial injury."

She gives me an incredulous look. "Surely, you're joking."

I issue a grumble of disagreement. "I assure you, I am not."

Her eyes flash with worry. She cups my cheek, turning my face to hers. "Am I really hurting you that badly?"

My heart clenches at her concern. She is only trying to help, and I am being a most ungrateful patient.

I could have lost her. The image of her being ripped away is burned into my memory. I failed her. I was supposed to keep her safe. If she were a Bear Shifter female, she would reject me now.

Instead, she patiently tends my wounds. And now, I have made her feel badly for doing so. So, despite my agony, I decide to try to coax a smile from her lips instead as I gently tease her. I arch a brow. "Is this the thanks I get for saving you? Now, you are trying to finish what the Griffin could not?"

Her jaw drops, but then a beautiful smile curves her lips when she notices the corners of my mouth tugging up. "You're joking with me?"

I search her eyes. "Would you prefer I be more serious?"

She cocks her head to the side. "No, it's just... it's the first time I've seen you joke."

She is right, and I realize I should remedy this.

"And? What do you think?"

Her lips curve into a stunning smile, and my heart stops momentarily. "I enjoy this side of you."

I cannot help but smile in return. My expression quickly falls, however, when she drags the cloth over my injuries again. I bite back a complaint, allowing her to continue.

"You need to let your body heal, Henrick. Maybe it would be best if you do not shift this evening."

"That may not be possible."

"Why?"

"Where there is one Griffin, there are often others."

All the color drains from her face. "There... could be more?"

I hate the fear in her eyes, so I move to reassure her. "I will protect you. I vow I will not fail you again."

She takes my hand. "You didn't fail me. Why do you say this?"

I lower my eyes. "The Griffin took you. You could have died because I was not fast enough. Because I did not—"

She presses a finger to my lips, silencing me. "Do not blame yourself. You saved me, Henrick. If *not* for you, I would be dead."

I say nothing.

If not for me, she would never have been taken in the first place.

If she were a Bear-Shifter female, she would already have turned from me because I failed to keep her from harm. For once, I'm relieved she is human, for it seems her kind doesn't judge as harshly.

A dozen emotions flicker across her features before she lies down next to me, shivering slightly as another breeze whips through the cave. I wrap an arm around her waist and tug her close, overjoyed when she snuggles into my body.

Although we have not yet mated, my body already instinctively recognizes her as mine. I long more than anything to claim her completely.

She tips her head back to gaze up at me. "You risked your life for me. Why?"

"Because you are my mate."

Clearly, she is not satisfied with my reply. "Yes, but I have not... truly been a mate to you. Not yet, anyway."

My ears prick up at the words *not yet*. On our wedding night, I was concerned that she might never wish to consummate our bond, but it seems she has begun reconsidering.

She continues. "So… why did you do it?"

"It is my duty, as your mate."

Even as the words leave my mouth, they do not seem right. Something about Anna intrigues me. Even had I never dreamed of her—even if I did not believe she was my fated one—I would still be drawn to her.

I always believed her kind was weak compared to mine, but seeing how brave she is and how fiercely she fought to defend me from the Griffin, I realize just how wrong I was.

"Your duty." She lowers her gaze. "Of course."

My words disappointed her, but I do not understand why. "You are upset."

"No."

We may have only recently met, but I already know her expressions well enough to recognize the lie that leaves her tongue. I want to ask for her truth, but I doubt she will relinquish it now.

She trusts me, but not enough to share all that is in her mind and heart.

CHAPTER 14

ANNA

I lower my head, considering his words. He believes it's his duty to keep me safe and take care of me, but he spoke nothing of love or emotion. Even so, I understand not every marriage begins with love. My parents have more of an... uneasy truce between them. At least Henrick and I share something closer to friendship.

Love may come later...

He places two fingers under my chin, tipping my face up. "What are you thinking about?"

It occurs to me I could lie, but I would rather be honest with him. After all, if a budding friendship and mutual understanding are all we can have, it should be based on honesty, at least.

"Our marriage and... my parents."

"I have heard your father does not honor the bond he has with your mother."

I blink, stunned by his blunt words. My father's proclivity

JESSICA GRAYSON & ARIA WINTER

for infidelity is known far and wide, but no one openly speaks of it. Not until now, that is. "That's true, yes."

"I vow not to do this to you, Anna. I bound myself to you under the winter's moon. I will honor that bonding with loyalty and devotion. Does this assuage your worries?"

Henrick has been kind to me—caring, even. He proved his devotion by coming to save me when it would have been easier to simply count me as dead. He nearly died while saving me. If that is not a strong start to a marriage and a show of loyalty and devotion, I do not know what is.

I take his hand and thread my fingers through his. "Yes, Henrick, it does."

We lock eyes for a moment before I rest my head on his shoulder, nestling into his arms. His warm, masculine scent surrounds me as I snuggle against him. At first, I was afraid of him, but I realize now that my fears are unfounded.

Henrick is simply blunt and his expressions are hard. But I have seen the tenderness beneath his cold exterior. He cares for me. Of this, I am certain. And because I know this, I feel safe in his arms.

I'm still not ready to take him into my bed, however. I know it is foolish, but I'd like there to be love between us before we share something so intimate. I am glad he has left this decision up to me. I am relieved he has no expectations beyond loyalty and devotion.

Those are easily given to a man like Henrick. Especially when I understand the lengths he would go to, to keep me safe.

And although we have not known each other long, I cannot deny the truth that has begun to take root deep in my heart. I am already beginning to fall in love with him.

CHAPTER 15

HENRICK

When I wake in the morning, Anna is still asleep in my arms. My gaze wanders down her form to the puncture wounds on her torso. My injuries have already closed, but humans cannot heal as quickly, it seems.

Guilt fills me as I study the angry red marks. I failed her yesterday. I could have so easily lost her. Had I not found her when I did, she would undoubtedly be dead.

The gods blessed me with my fated one, and I have already proven myself entirely unworthy of such a gift.

Gently, I brush the hair back from her face as need burns through me like fire. I long more than anything to claim her completely. She is the most beautiful female I have ever seen.

She is kind and caring, and devoted to me in a way that I had not expected. I'd thought my inability to love would keep her at a distance, but it seems I was pleasantly wrong.

A sharp pain stabs at my chest, reminding me of the ice

that surrounds my heart. The curse placed upon me by the Snow Queen.

Although the curse prevents me from loving her, I do *care* for Anna. I only pray it is enough for my mate.

I am hesitant to wake her as she lies so trustingly in my arm. I wish I did not have to wake her, but we must leave now that the first light is here. We need to rejoin our party.

I instructed Aurick and a few others to search for her, with the agreement that we'd all meet at a set location within the next few days.

Anna blinks sleepily at me before jerking up and hissing sharply through her teeth at the sudden movement. "Is everything all right?"

"Yes, but we should leave to find my guards." I dart a glance at the marks again. "Do you feel well enough to travel?"

She nods, and her attention drops to my chest, her mouth drifting open in shock when she notices my wounds are completely closed. "How is this possible?"

"My kind heal quickly."

"I'm so glad you're better." A faint smile crests her lips. "I was worried."

I'm not sure whether to be touched or offended by her statement. If she were a female Bear Shifter, she would think me weak. But as I scan her slight, delicate form, I realize I cannot judge her by the same standards as my people. Humans are different, and I am still learning their ways.

As she moves to retrieve her clothing, I appreciatively inspect her bare form. Now that I am well, my *stav* hardens painfully with the desire to join my body to hers, but I force myself to settle.

She does not want me... and she may never want me.

Once she is finished dressing, I shift forms, and she climbs onto my back. The path along the mountain cliff wall is steep and treacherous, but I am accustomed to dangerous travel. I have scaled these mountains many times before. It is much faster to take the mountain pass than to travel the valley route by carriage, which can add three to four days to a journey.

Her smaller hands cling tightly to my fur as I navigate the mountain. When we reach a much wider trail, she relaxes slightly.

"It is not much farther."

"Thank the gods."

We travel in relative silence before she finally feels comfortable enough to speak once we reach a flatter stretch. "I'm glad we talked last night."

"You are?"

"Yes."

"Good."

"What about your family? Your parents? Did they… have a good relationship?"

"No."

She's silent for a moment before asking, "Why do you say that?"

"My father held to the old ways."

"The old ways? What are those?"

"He wanted my mother. She was betrothed to another. He challenged her suitor and killed him in battle, thus winning her hand." Anna inhales sharply, but I continue. "She never forgave him. There was never any love between them. He took her whenever he wanted. She gave him many cubs but hated him for it. Each time he mounted her, it was a conquering, not a union."

Anna stills on my back. I turn my gaze to her and find her mouth agape. "That's… it must have been awful growing up knowing that."

"I pitied my mother. And I vowed I would never do that to my mate."

"That's why…" She trails off.

"Why what?"

"Why you promised not to touch me until I ask."

I bow my head in acknowledgment.

"You are a good man," she says softly, and my chest swells with pride. "Even if you are a bit gruff and speak bluntly."

I tip my head up. "It is the way of the North."

A soft laugh escapes her. "I think I'm beginning to understand that."

CHAPTER 16

ANNA

Despite my light teasing with him, my heart clenches as I think about what he just shared with me. I cannot imagine how hard it must have been for Henrick, growing up in such a family. For all that he is fierce, blunt, and a bit… odd, I feel sorry for him. I lean forward, resting my head against the back of his neck.

Henrick is a good man. Much more so than I first believed.

"Thank you for giving me time," I tell him.

"Time?"

"To fall in love with you before we join."

He stills, and something about the way he tenses fills me with concern. "Is love… important to you?"

"Yes, it is," I reply honestly. "Do… Bear Shifters not love?"

I wait anxiously for him to answer. I know his outer demeanor is rather cold, but I've seen what it hides—a caring and kind man who is protective of me. A man who would do anything to keep me safe and by his side.

Before he can answer, movement in the distance catches my eye, startling me. I relax as soon as I recognize Henrick's guards. Aurick comes bounding up to greet us in his two-legged form. "My King. My Queen." He lowers his massive head. "It is good to see you safely returned."

"Fetch healing supplies and bandages," Henrick commands. "The Queen has been injured."

Aurick's face visibly pales a moment before he rushes back to the camp.

We follow him back to a large, plateaued area, on the side of the mountain, and Engrid rushes toward me. I note all the tents have been set up while the guards waited for us to return.

I slide off Henrick's back, and she wraps her arms tightly around me. "I was so afraid I'd never see you again." Her voice hitches. "Thank the gods you are alive."

"I'm fine. What about you?" I ask. "Are you all right?"

She nods, and I do not miss the way her gaze sweeps to Aurick, her cheeks flushing. "Aurick has been watching over me ever since the Griffin attack."

I smile at Henrick's bodyguard. "Thank you."

He bows again. "It is my honor, my Queen."

Another guard walks up to him, bowing low as he presents a small wooden box.

Aurick lifts the latch and inside are containers of—what I assume must be—healing salves and bandages. He looks to me. "If you would remove your clothing, I will treat your wounds."

Hot embarrassment floods my cheeks. I know nudity is nothing to Bear Shifters, but I'm not comfortable with the idea of being unclothed in front of Henrick's men.

As if sensing my hesitation, Henrick steps forward. "Bring the supplies to our tent."

Aurick bows before he and Engrid follow us to the tent.

86

When we enter, Henrick guides me to the bedroll, while Aurick sets down the box of supplies. He turns to them. "Leave us."

Engrid gives me a questioning look. "But, my Lady, I—"

"It's fine, Engrid," I reassure her. "My husband will tend me."

Her eyes dart to Henrick before she turns to leave with Aurick.

Once we're alone, I remove my dress. I love that he recognized my discomfort and immediately addressed it by bringing me to the tent to treat my injuries.

Normally, I'd be shy about undressing in front of him, but after last night, I have no reservations about being unclothed in his presence. He is my husband after all, and he has already said he will not touch me until I ask him.

Henrick's eyes travel over my body, but instead of desire I see something akin to guilt reflecting behind them. "Forgive me," he murmurs, tracing his fingers lightly across my skin, near my wounds. "It is my fault you were injured."

I take his hand. "I already told you: There is nothing to forgive, Henrick."

"I failed to protect you." He clenches his jaw. "If you were a Bear-Shifter female you would reject me, and be well within your right to."

I cup his cheek, and a smile crests my lips as I decide to tease him. "Well, then it's a good thing you did not marry a Bear Shifter, then, isn't it?"

He arches a teasing brow in return. "I suppose you are right."

When he is finished dressing my wound, he holds a long, fur coat out to me. I slip my arms through the sleeves. Once it's secured over my shoulders, he tightens the belt around my waist to make sure I'm covered and warm.

Just that extra bit of care melts my heart.

When he is finished, he instructs his guards to tear down our camp.

"We're leaving?" I ask when he turns back to me.

"I will not risk camping here when there could be more Griffins nearby. You will not be safe until we are off this mountain. We must reach Kyruna before dark. We will rest once we get there."

I've never been this far from home, but from what I recall of my study of this kingdom, Kyruna is still quite far away—several hours at least.

The ride here was tiring, and my sides ache where my wounds are still healing. Having to hold so tightly makes my muscles and injuries that much sorer, but I know he is right. I'm eager to get off this mountain. The memory of the Griffin attack is burned in my mind, and I have no wish to remain here any longer, so I anchor my resolve.

"All right."

Henrick refuses to allow me to help pack up our camp. So, instead, I take a moment to speak with Engrid.

She takes my hand, squeezing it gently. "What happened?" she asks. "How did you survive?"

As I tell her the details of my story, her eyes widen in shock.

After I'm finished, she hugs me close. "Thank the gods he found you when he did." She pulls back. "As soon as you were taken, the king went after you. He told his guards he would either save you or die trying."

Shame fills me as I think on how I doubted him. "I thought he would not bother," I admit. "After all, we are newly married and barely know each other."

"He cares for you, my Lady. He is a good man. They all are, from what I have observed." Her gaze drifts to Aurick in the distance. "Aurick told me that Bear Shifters mate for life. They are devoted to their mates."

I did not know this. From the way Henrick said he didn't care if I'd had any lovers before him, I assumed he'd probably had many himself.

Engrid leans in and whispers. "But Aurick also told me something else. Something I believe he did not truly intend to share."

"What was it?"

"He said that they feared Henrick would never marry because of his curse."

"What curse?"

She shakes her head. "I do not know. When I asked him about it, he only said that Henrick had been cursed by the Snow Queen to never know love."

I inhale sharply. The Snow Queen is a powerful blood witch, and everyone fears her.

"What happened? Why was he cursed?"

"He made a bargain to try to save his older brother, but the witch betrayed him. She cursed him, and allowed his brother to die anyway."

I frown. "I did not know. Henrick didn't tell me anything about this."

"Aurick says he does not speak of it… that he refuses to."

Engrid starts to tell me more, but Henrick interrupts us. "Come," he says. "We must leave before the weather grows worse."

I hug Engrid again before she heads back to Aurick. I notice the way he smiles brightly at her as she walks over to him. It seems they are both smitten with each other.

Henrick and his men shift back into their bear forms. I climb onto his back once more, and we continue our trek down the mountain.

The wind is stronger on this side of the pass. It whips through my hair and claws at my frame as if trying to rip me from Henrick's back. I dig my fingers into his fur, afraid I might fall.

My thoughts drift to Henrick's curse. I desperately want to ask him about it, but I'm not sure how to begin. Especially since Aurick told her that he never speaks of it.

She said the curse would somehow prevent him from knowing love, but I wonder what it entails. If the Snow Queen thought it would keep someone from falling for him, her curse has already failed. I've known him less than a handful of days and I'm already halfway in love with my new husband.

I'll have to find a way to ask him about it. Maybe once we reach Arnafell, after we have settled in...

Small rocks scrape beneath his powerful body, echoing along the wall as they tumble off the mountainside, and ripping me from my thoughts. I strain to listen as they fall, trying to gauge how far up we are by how long they take to strike the base of the mountain somewhere below us.

The wind howls around the mountain. I pull the hood over my head against the chill, but the cold is biting and bone-deep. We have winter in my father's kingdom, but I've never experienced anything like this.

My thoughts turn to Henrick's comment about how Arnafell is always covered in snow. However, I suppose the cold is like everything else in life; one can become accustomed to it given enough time and exposure.

At least, this is what I hope.

As we descend below the cloud cover, I scan the land below. Ice and snow blanket the landscape as far as the eye can see. In the distance, I notice the white-capped rooftops of what can only be the city of Kyruna.

A large, stone wall surrounds the city. Dark smoke puffs from the chimneys of houses and businesses. A waterfall from the mountain spills into a large river below that winds its way straight through the heart of the town.

"That is Kyruna," Henrick says. "We will spend the night there and continue to Arnafell tomorrow."

I cannot deny I'm looking forward to sleeping in an actual bed this evening and perhaps even enjoying the warmth of a fire. My stomach growls in protest, and I realize I haven't eaten since this morning.

Henrick must have overheard because he glances over his shoulder. "We will eat first then rest."

As we trudge through the snow and ice, I press against Henrick's back, burying my face into his fur for warmth every now and then when I can no longer feel my nose. I'm quickly coming to associate his scent—a heady mix of fresh rain and forest—with warmth and comfort.

The deep reverberation of a horn sounds in the distance, and I lift my head toward Kyruna. Guards gather along the wall surrounding the city, standing at attention as their king and his men approach.

The wall is much taller than I could tell from a distance, and the entrance is guarded by two massive, silver doors. The sigil of the bear—Henrick's banner—is engraved across the center, mighty and proud. As we approach, they begin to swing open. The sound of ice cracking from around the edges as they do, tells me the doors are normally kept shut.

I wonder what it is they are meant to keep out.

I make a mental note to ask Henrick later when we're alone.

We make our way through the city on a teeming thoroughfare. It seems the king is as popular here as he was in Islo.

The cobblestone streets appear clean and neatly kept. Lamp posts line the walkways, casting a soft warm glow throughout the city. Couples and families dressed in heavy cloaks and fur hats gather on either side of our procession, each of them bowing low as we pass.

Henrick walks up to a woman who I assume must be the city's leader. He carefully lowers himself for me to slide off his back. She holds out a folded robe to him, and he shifts forms.

I note he makes sure to create the illusion of wearing pants. My gaze travels over his bare torso. The hard plans of muscle rippling as he slides the robe over his shoulders.

"Mayor Kristan," he addresses her, and she drops into a bow. "This is my queen, Anna."

Her green eyes widen slightly as they meet mine and she bows again, her long, dark braid slipping over her shoulder as she does so. "I am honored to meet you, my queen."

I dip my chin in subtle greeting. "And I, you."

"We will be spending the night here before leaving for Arnafell in the morning."

A wide smile splits her face. "It is an honor to host you, Your Majesties." She gestures to a man standing beside her. His bright blue eyes and his tall height make me wonder if he's a Bear Shifter, but I'm not entirely sure. "Urvik will take you to your accommodations as soon as you are ready."

Henrik holds out his arm to me. I loop mine through his, and he steps forward to address the people.

"People of Kyruna, I present to you Queen Anna of Arnafell."

The crowd erupts in a series of joyous cheers, and I cannot help the smile that crests my lips at this warm reception. It's such a vast difference from when we would visit various cities in my father's kingdom.

My father fears his people, and we were constantly surrounded by protection whenever we would travel with him. Whereas, Henrick and his guards appear completely at ease.

Henrick instructs his men to begin unloading trunks full of gold and silver coins—a gift for the city.

Mayor Kristan has tears in her eyes when she addresses him. "My King, we cannot thank you enough."

"There is no need to thank me," Henrick replies. "It is the least I can do for Kyruna. Your city is the northern line of defense for Arnafell. Long have we remained safe from the Snow Queen and her minions, thanks in part to your efforts."

A chill runs down my spine at mention of the Snow Queen. I had not realized the Kyruna bordered her territory.

"It is our honor to protect this part of the kingdom, my King."

Now, I understand the reason for the defensive wall that surrounds the city.

Our presence has caused quite a stir here. Minstrels arrive and begin playing as citizens bring out tables with large pots of warm soups and wooden platters of freshly baked bread. The delicious smell of beef stew and dough wafts through the air.

I turn to Henrick and whisper, "Do the people always greet you this way?"

He nods and guides me toward one of the tables. One of the townsfolk ladles stew in two bowls and passes them to us. If my father were here, he'd have handed this off to a taster to check for poison, but not Henrick.

He does not fear his people's vengeance like my father does, perhaps because he is a good, fair king who does not have to worry about insurgence or unrest.

This only reaffirms my good impression of him so far. He is a ruler beloved by his people.

On a bench not far away, I notice Engrid sitting beside Aurick, the two laughing as they enjoy a bowl of warm soup.

Children rush toward us, and Henrick drops to one knee, bending down further until his face is level with theirs.

"King Henrick," one child begins, her brown eyes full of wonder, "will you transform into a bear again? Please."

"Of course, little one."

He sets down his bowl then shifts in an instant.

The children gasp, and their tiny faces light with joy. I watch in awe as a few of the children shift into cubs, as well. Henrick growls then pretends to chase them, the group giggling as they run.

Beside me, the Mayor smiles as we watch them all interact. One of the cubs trips and falls. The Mayor cries out, "Torek!"

She rushes toward him, and I follow. She drops to her knees and pulls his head into her lap. His eyes are bright with unshed tears. "Are you all right?"

He lifts his paw, and she takes it in her hand, tracing her fingers across the pads. "It's just sprained." She lifts her head. "Where is your father?"

"Here," a voice booms behind us. I spin and am confronted by bright, blue eyes, immediately recognizing Urvik. He kneels and scoops his son into his arms. He places a tender kiss on the Mayor's forehead. "I'll take him home, my love."

Another cub rushes up to us. He shifts back into two-legged form, his expression anxious as he addresses the Mayor. "Will he be all right, Mother?"

She smiles. "Of course, Larik."

The little boy turns to me and smiles. "Are you really the queen?"

"Yes, I am."

He straightens, tipping his chin up with pride. "I'm going to be one of the king's guards someday."

I grin. "And I'm sure you will make an excellent guard."

"Thank you, my queen," he replies, practically beaming with joy at the compliment.

With that, he skips off to play with the other children. I turn to the Mayor and find her gaze tracking her son, a warm smile on her face. I've heard humans intermarry with shifters, but this is the first couple I've seen. In my father's kingdom, it is rare for any non-humans to settle.

I'm exhausted from our journey, but I have so many questions I want to ask the Mayor about her relationship with her husband.

"How did you and your husband meet?"

"We grew up together." A wistful smile crests her lips. "His parents wanted him to pick a traditional mate, but... we've been in love since we were sixteen. It was never a question if we'd marry—only when."

Her gaze drifts to Henrick. "There used to be so much strife between humans and shifters in the kingdom under Henrick's father. He believed in tradition, you know. He barely tolerated the presence of humans in his kingdom, but when Henrick ascended the throne, he changed all that. Made things much easier for those of us who are not... traditional."

I did not know this about my husband. Before our marriage, I had never even visited the kingdom of Arnafell. I heard stories of the Bear Shifters that make their homes here, but I'd never seen one before I met Henrick.

I always thought of them as fierce and terrifying warriors. However, watching Henrick and his men play with the children and laugh with the people of Kyruna and Islo, I know now that the tales I heard were exaggerated. Henrick and his guards are good people.

"It is wonderful to know that our king has finally found a mate," she adds. "We were beginning to worry that he might end up alone. He has searched far and wide for a queen."

Her gaze drifts to Henrick as he talks to some of the

townspeople across the way. "It has been a long time since I have seen our king smile so much," she adds.

As if somehow knowing we are speaking of him, Henrick's head snaps toward me. When his eyes meet mine, he flashes a devastatingly handsome smile that makes my heart flutter.

He walks over to me, and the Mayor steps back to give us some privacy. "Would you like something else to eat?"

I shake my head. "I'm so full I couldn't possibly take another bite."

"You are tired. You should rest, Anna."

I love how attentive he is to my needs. My father was never this way with my mother.

Exhausted from the events of yesterday and the trek here, I struggle to stifle another yawn.

I frown. "How did you know?"

"You have yawned at least three times over the past ten minutes."

I laugh. "You were watching me? Keeping count?"

"You are my mate. Of course, I was watching you. I always watch you. You are mine to care for, Anna."

Warmth fills me at his words. I blink up at him, unsure of how to respond.

"Come. Let us go to bed," he says. "We have a long day ahead of us tomorrow."

We start to walk away, but Aurick comes over to us. "My King, I need to speak with you."

Henrick's eyes flash back to me, but I wave him off. "It's all right. I'll go on ahead."

He dips his chin, and I turn to leave with the Mayor.

She leads me down a walkway leading away from the city center along the river's edge. A thick layer of ice covers the surface, and I watch a few of the kids, including the Mayor's son, Larik, slide and skitter as they play on the ice.

Flakes of snow twirl and dance on the breeze as the sound of the children's laughter fills the air.

This really is a lovely place, even if it is a bit colder than I'd like.

I turn to the Mayor. "It will be lovely to sleep in a warm bed this evening."

She smiles. "I believe you will like the rooms we've made ready. They are—"

A terrified scream rings out from one of the children. Alarm bursts through me when I spin toward the river and watch as the Mayor's son falls through the ice.

"Larik!" the Mayor shrieks, rushing toward the river.

Panic floods my veins as he hangs onto the broken edge of the ice, wailing in terror as the river tries to drag him under.

Her husband—Urvik—rushes onto the ice, but his weight is too much. A sharp crack cuts the air, and fine fissures spread beneath him like a spider's web upon the icy surface.

He skids to a halt at the river's edge, frozen with indecision.

Of the few adults nearby, I realize I am the smallest. "I'll go."

"No!" Urvik shouts. "I will—"

"You're too heavy. I'm not."

Without waiting for him to reply, I carefully step onto the ice. Horror spurs me on as the Larik's voice begins to weaken. He struggles to hold on to the edge, his face, hands, and lips turning blue from the cold.

Another crack slices beneath me, and I still as the ice shift slightly under my feet.

"My Queen!" the Mayor wails behind me.

"I need a rope," I yell over my shoulder.

I cautiously kneel and begin crawling slowly across the

ice, hoping to spread my weight out enough that I won't break through the surface.

"Hold on, Larik. I'm coming."

He barely manages to lift his head, his entire body shuddering with frost and terror.

I have almost reached him when Henrick's voice stops me. "Anna, wait!"

"There's no time, Henrick. Just find me some rope. Throw it to us. Please."

"Hurry!" he forces out, and I hear a flurry of activity behind me that I can only hope is someone finding me what I need to save Larik before the water and ice claim him.

My body is shivering as I inch toward him. When I finally get close enough, I stretch my arm forward, taking his small hand.

"Here's a rope, Anna!"

I recognize Henrick's voice, followed quickly by a slap on the ice as the rope drops to my right.

With my left hand, I grab Larik, and with my right, I grasp the rope then wind it around my hand and wrist. Finally, I carefully begin to pull Larik up, out of the freezing water.

Another sharp crack sounds as fissures appear beneath me. The ice shifts again, and I only have a moment to draw in a deep breath before it gives way, plunging me into the icy current.

The sensation of a million needles stabbing my skin is excruciating, but I force myself to hold onto the rope and Larik. Cold water steals my breath, and my body begins to lock up, refusing to move.

Gritting my teeth, I struggle to remain conscious even as the dark void beckons me to fall into its welcoming embrace.

My eyes jerk open when I feel a sharp tug on my body. I squeeze them shut again as my skin drags over something cold and hard. In the back of my mind, I register the icy ground, but I can neither move nor do anything but hold on to the rope.

A voice calls my name. Gathering my strength, I open my eyes and find ice-blue ones staring down at me. "Anna." Henrick cups my cheek, clutching me to his chest. "Anna, you have to stay awake."

I reach up and touch his face. "Henrick," I barely manage to gasp before my head falls back, and I fall into darkness.

CHAPTER 17

HENRICK

Larik's father gathers him in his arms as I pull Anna to my chest. I cup her cheek, turning her face to me. Her eyelids flutter.

Fear paralyzes me, and my heart hammers violently in my chest. "Anna, you have to stay awake."

She reaches a trembling hand up to touch my face. "Henrick, I'm so cold."

"Find a Healer!"

Two people rush forward. One man treats the child while a woman stops in front of me. She studies Anna for a moment before lifting her green eyes to mine. "We need to get her warm. Now."

"This way, my king!"

I follow the voice without hesitation. One of the townsfolk leads me to an inn. He guides me up the stairs and into the first room at the top of the landing.

A large bed in one corner is piled high with blankets and

furs. I'm relieved to notice the fire already burning in the hearth, the roaring flames warming the room.

"We have to get her out of those clothes," the Healer demands.

Immediately, I extend my claws, slicing through the fabric until it falls to the floor with a wet slap, leaving Anna naked and shivering in my arms.

I gently lay her on the bed, covering her with layers of furs.

The Healer pulls several vials from her satchel, and I watch curiously as she combines them into one. She leans over Anna, and carefully tips up her head, holding the vial to her lips. "You must drink this, my queen. It will help."

Anna gives her a weak nod.

The Healer carefully pours the liquid in her mouth, and I watch Anna drink with bated breath. Once some of the color returns to her face and the blue tinge to her lips retreats in favor of their normal pink hue, I exhale my relief.

"You should move her closer to the fire," the Healer advises.

Gently gathering Anna up, I carry her to the fireplace. Shifting instantly, I lie down on the floor, pulling her toward me to drape one arm over her torso. She closes her eyes. Instinctively, she nestles against me for warmth.

"How long will it take for your medicine to work?"

"It is already working. Do not worry, my king; the tincture tends to make people drowsy. When she wakes in the morning, she will be fine."

"Thank you." I bow my head in a gesture of profound gratitude. "Will you come back to check on her in the morning?"

"Of course, my King." The Healer bows.

Aurick stands in the doorway, watching as she leaves, then turns to me. "My king."

"We are fine," I tell him. "Take the room next door so you are nearby if I need you."

He bows and turns to leave.

A strange ache throbs in my chest when I curl protectively around her. I'm acutely aware of how much smaller she is, and how fragile and helpless she seems tonight. Perhaps this is the cause of the pull I feel to protect and watch over her—the reason my chest feels tight as I study her face, waiting for any sign she will awaken.

Strangely, I long to see her lovely, hazel eyes. I do not understand why she produces these feelings in me, but I realize something even more important: I cannot ignore them.

CHAPTER 18

ANNA

As my mind slowly awakens, I'm surrounded by warmth. I breathe deep of Henrick's masculine scent and open my eyes to find his ice-blue ones searching mine in concern. "How do you feel?" he asks softly.

"Tired," I murmur. I dart a glance around the room. The soft, orange glow of the fire is the only light in this space. I'm snuggled against Henrick, in his bear form, and he's so warm I wish I could stay here like this forever.

Snow falls heavily outside the window, and I notice it is dark. "How long was I asleep?"

"You slept all night after the Healer tended you, and all through the day."

I frown. "You... stayed with me all that time?"

He gently nuzzles my temple. In the blink of an eye, he shifts into his human form and hugs me tightly to his chest. "I thought the river would take you, Anna. I was so afraid I would lose you."

"You saved me, Henrick. I'm fine."

He pulls back, tipping my face up by my chin. Devotion and anger war across his features. "You should not have risked your life like that. You are the queen. You—"

"What was I supposed to do—let Larik drown? Freeze to death? I was the only person who could go so far onto the ice without—"

"You could have died," he cuts me off, his expression thunderous.

"But I didn't."

"But you *could* have, Anna." Clenching his jaw, he looks away. "I watched you fall through the ice. The river swallowed you, and I thought you were dead."

I touch his face, drawing his eyes back to mine. "Henrick, I'm fine. Truly. Why are you so upset? Everything is all right now."

He reaches out and brushes a stray tendril of hair behind my ear, his expression a strange mixture of sadness and devotion as he surveys my face. "I have almost lost you twice now. I—"

A loud knock on the door startles us both. "Enter!" he calls out.

Aurick walks in, and I note how Henrick makes sure to shield my partially clothed body from his view.

"My King." Aurick bows low. "Forgive my intrusion, but Engrid is requesting to see the queen."

I glance over Henrick's shoulder and smile when I notice Engrid standing behind Aurick.

"My Lady!" she exclaims. "You are awake!"

I wrap one of the furs tight around my body, and Henrick helps me to stand.

Engrid rushes forward and embraces me warmly. "Thank the gods you are well." She pulls back just enough to appraise me. "Your color is fully returned. Tell me: are you hungry? Thirsty?"

I shake my head. "No, but I wouldn't turn down a warm bath."

She smiles. "I'll have one drawn for you."

Henrick turns to me. "I will retrieve some food and drink for you, while you bathe."

As I relax in the warm bath, Engrid sits on a chair beside me. "It was brave of you to risk your life for the child," she says.

I do not think of myself as brave. "Anyone would have done the same."

"It is all everyone has been talking about," she adds. "It seems you have won both the admiration and love of the people, and the deep respect of Henrick's guards." She grins. "They are calling you a true Queen of the North."

"They are?"

She nods. "And the king... he is so devoted to you, my Lady." She places her hand over her heart. "He refused to leave your side even for a moment while you were unconscious." She releases a dreamy sigh. "It was so romantic the way he cared for you."

Happiness blooms in my chest.

When I'm finished bathing, I dress and we head downstairs to a large dining hall. It seems this inn is used for big gatherings in this city. Several of Henrick's men observe as I pass. Crossing their arms over their chests, they bow low.

The dining hall is full of people. I allow my gaze to travel over the room, scanning the several long wooden tables as I search for my husband. I spot him immediately across the way, standing next to the massive fireplace. The roaring fire providing warmth and soft lighting throughout the space.

Henrick's head whips toward me and he smiles. I do not know how he always seems to know when I'm searching for him, but he does. As I make my way toward him, several of the townspeople observe in silence as I pass, their eyes alight with a strange mixture of curiosity and awe.

Just before I reach Henrick, the Mayor and her husband intercept me. "We do not know how to thank you," she says. "You saved our son."

"We owe you a life debt," Urvik adds. "If not for your bravery, Larik would be dead."

I start to ask how he is, when he and his brother move from behind their parents. Larik smiles up at me. I kneel, and embrace him warmly. "I am so glad you are all right."

He grins. "Thank you for saving me, my Queen."

Henrick walks up beside us, resting a hand on my shoulder. "I have promised Larik a place on your personal guard someday, if he still wishes, when he is older," Henrick says.

Larik beams a moment before he drops to one knee and bows low. "I vow to protect and defend you, my queen."

I smile at him. "I'm sure you will make an excellent guard someday. But only if you still desire this when you are older. I will not hold you to it, if you decide upon doing something else with your life." I give his parents a meaningful look. I do not want their son to feel bound to honor a promise made in his childhood. "All right?"

He grins. "All right."

Henrick and I take a seat at one of the tables, and he moves close to me on the bench. So close that the warmth of his body radiates to mine. We talk back and forth with the Mayor and husband. They truly are a lovely couple.

As the night wears on, he wraps a possessive arm around my waist and I find myself leaning into him, breathing deeply of his warm, masculine scent.

It's strange how familiar he already is to me. I'd heard that shared trauma can bind people very quickly, and it seems this is true. After the events of the past few days, I feel close to him in a way that I never expected would happen so soon.

Exhaustion hits me like a giant wave, and I cover my mouth to stifle a yawn.

Henrick turns to me. "You are tired. We should return to our rooms to rest."

I love how attentive he is to my needs. "All right," I agree.

CHAPTER 19

ANNA

When we reach our room, he makes sure the fire is stoked and the flames are burning brightly to warm the space. I lie down in bed, and he gently lays several fur blankets over me then moves to the door.

He drops one of the furs onto the floor and settles on it, turning his back to me.

"What are you doing?"

"Going to sleep. We have a long day ahead of us tomorrow. It is a full day's journey to the castle."

I sit up in bed, pulling the furs back and placing my palm on the mattress. "You may sleep in the bed with me." His eyes widen, so I quickly add, "But only to sleep, nothing more."

He stands and walks toward me. The mattress dips as he settles into bed, massive even in human form.

Resting my head on his shoulder, I drape my arm across his chest and search his face. "Is this all right?"

"Yes." His brows furrow. "You are growing accustomed to me, are you not?"

I snort, thinking back to when he said he would gentle me like a horse. I was upset then, though I realize now he meant no offense. He is simply blunt. "I suppose I am."

He places his hand over mine on his chest.

"You are different than I imagined you would be," I murmur.

"Better or worse?" he asks, arching a brow.

"Much better." I laugh softly.

He cups my chin. "You do not regret taking me as your husband?"

His piercing blue eyes search mine as he waits for my answer. I could so easily lose myself in their depths. "No," I answer honestly.

His lips curve up in a gorgeous smile.

"I have something I want to ask you."

His expression turns serious again. "What is it?"

I hesitate a moment, unsure how to begin. But then I remember he has asked me to be truthful with him. "Is it true you are cursed?"

His brow furrows deeply. "Yes."

I wait patiently for him to continue, but he remains silent. After a moment, I ask. "Will you tell me about it?"

He clenches his jaw and nods. "My older brother—Verick —fell ill. He was dying and the only way to save him was to make a bargain with a blood witch—the Snow Queen."

"What happened?"

"I went with my friend—Prince Malak—to her lands."

I frown. "Prince Malak of Winterhold—the Wolf Shifter?"

He nods. I'd thought Bear Shifters and Wolf Shifters were natural enemies but it seems I was wrong.

"Malak is a good male, despite his family," he says, as if reading my thoughts. "We were once as close as brothers. He tried to stop me from seeking help from the Snow Queen, but I was desperate to save my brother, and I refused to listen."

"So, then what happened?"

"She asked for my heart in exchange to heal his. I was young and foolish. I thought she literally wanted the beating heart from my chest, but what she wanted was my undying love and devotion." He shakes his head. "When I realized what she meant, I was honest with her... I explained that I could not offer her something that was false."

I inhale sharply, imagining how she must have taken his blunt and truthful words.

"It is the way of the North to speak truth," he says. "I could not offer her a lie. So, I asked for a different bargain." He pauses. "Instead, she became enraged—angry that I'd rejected her advances. She said if I could not love her, I would never know love."

His blue eyes meet mine. "She froze my heart; encased it in ice with her dark magic so that I cannot love. Because I had angered her, she did not heal my brother, and he died." He swallows hard. "I failed him."

Tears gather in the corner of my eyes as I squeeze his hand. "I'm so sorry, Henrick."

He shakes his head. "The fault is mine. I should have known better than to deal with her in the first place, but I was desperate to save Verick."

For a man who cannot love, he is beloved by everyone who knows him—his people and his guards.

He turns his gaze to me. "I had thought our marriage would be one of simple politics to unite our kingdoms and ensure no further discord between our people. But you told me that love is important to you. If you wish to annul our marriage, I will not keep you against your will, Anna. But I would know now if you wish to leave."

Even as I consider his words, I already know my answer. He may be incapable of love, but the level of care, attention, and tenderness he has shown me in only a few days has already made me begin falling in love with him.

Henrick treats me as if I am the most important thing in the world. And yet, I wonder if I can truly be happy knowing he can never return my love.

I do know one thing for certain: I am willing to find out. And I am also determined to try to help him. "Is there a way to break the curse?"

"If there is, I have not found it," he says soberly. "I have tried. Many times."

My uncle's family was cursed by a blood witch, but he found a way around it. When my father asked him how he did this, he told him that every curse has the potential to be broken. You simply have to figure out how to break the inner workings of the spell, unraveling it from the inside out.

"Why did you marry me?" I ask, curious to understand his motivations when he knew that love would not be possible between us.

"I have need of a queen to help carry the burden of rule," he says. "And I need heirs." He lifts a thoughtful gaze to the ceiling. "You are not the first one I offered my hand to."

His words are like a slap to the face, even as my fledgling heart begins to shatter. I know I should not be surprised that he pursued others, but it hurts to know I am not his first choice.

He continues. "But I believe you are the most beautiful." He pauses. "And the bravest, as well. Any cubs that result of our joining will be blessed with a fierce mother."

My heart simultaneously plummets and soars. Now that I know he cannot love, my mind understands that it would be wiser to leave now before I fall even further. But my heart insists that I stay.

At his mention of children, I realize that it is not just my life at stake, as well. How would it be for children to grow up with a father that could not truly love them? Yes, he would be devoted and loyal, just as he is to me, but would it be enough?

I'm not even sure it would be enough for me alone.

My mind wars with my heart, insisting I should leave now. But when Henrick tucks the blanket around my shoulders to make sure I'm warm, and he tightens his arms around me, my heart wins the argument. "I will stay with you, Henrick."

As his blue eyes stare deep into mine, I steel my determination. I will find a way to melt the ice around Henrick's heart and break his curse.

CHAPTER 20

ANNA

The glow of morning light filters in through the windows. I'm completely enveloped in warmth with Henrick curled protectively around me. I inhale his masculine scent and turn in his arms to face him.

With his eyes still closed, he appears so peaceful. Gone are all the hard lines of his face and his usually severe expression. I reach out and gently touch him, tracing my fingers over his sharp brow and nose. It's strange to think that, only days ago, I did not know him, and I had no husband.

We've been through so much in such a short amount of time. Despite his blunt manners and stoic personality, I cannot ignore the sharp tug in my heart when he opens his eyes and gives me a sleepy smile.

"Good morning," I whisper.

He leans in, gently nuzzling my temple, the gesture so intimate it makes my face heat. "Good morning, my queen." He sits up. "We should leave as soon as possible. I did not mean to sleep for so long."

Quickly, I stand and make my way to the cleansing room. "I'll be fast. I promise."

He opens his mouth, and I suspect he's going to protest that I do not need to bathe this morning, so I cut him off by adding, "We'll eat breakfast on the way."

His jaw snaps shut, and I close the door behind me.

When we head downstairs into the small courtyard in front of the inn, several of the townspeople have gathered to bid us farewell.

The Mayor steps forward with her bear-shifter husband and sons. They bow low before us. "We can never repay you for what you did for us, my Queen. We are forever grateful to you."

They told me this last night, and I'm still not sure how to respond. I did what anyone would have done in my situation. No decent person would allow a child to drown if they could help it.

Henrick must sense I'm at a loss for words because he steps forward. "And we appreciate you guarding and protecting the borders of Arnafell."

The Mayor sweeps into a bow. "Of course, my King."

The other townsfolk who have gathered bow, as well. When they straighten, they chant, "Long live King Henrick. Long live Queen Anna."

Henrick shifts, and I climb onto his back. I note Engrid is not far behind us with Aurick.

Even if I was not already falling for him by myself, her words about how he reacted when I was taken by the Griffin, and how he refused to leave my side when I was unconscious only made my heart open to him even more.

I noted again, this morning, how Aurick's eyes always

seemed to be upon her. I cannot still the jealousy inside me that he is not cursed. She could give herself over to him completely and I have no doubt he would return her love.

Whereas I must be careful. I cannot allow myself to surrender to these feelings Henrick stirs deep in my soul. If I do, and we are unable to break his curse…

I force myself to push my dark thoughts aside. Our marriage is still new and nothing has happened that cannot be taken back. If I decide I am unhappy, our bonding can still be annulled. I do not want to do this to him, but I also recognize that I have to protect my heart.

Right now, his loyalty, devotion, and caring are enough. But part of me fears that I will reach a point where it no longer is. And when that time comes, I will have to make a decision: do I give up on him? Or do I stay and make it work?

As we leave town, the snow-covered fields give way to the white-capped trees of a dense forest.

Time seems to pass by much faster today as I think on everything I have learned about my new husband.

The sun hangs low on the horizon, and I wonder how close we are to Arnafell.

While passing under the thick tree canopy, only bare slivers of light penetrate the thick cover, casting sinister shadows all around us. I pull my coat tighter around me, not to guard against the chill but the fear of what may await us in these woods.

Henrick always insists that we not travel at night, and I wonder if there is a reason. Does something terrible lurk in these woods?

Without warning, Henrick stills. His entire body goes tense beneath me. Fear spikes through my chest when I notice the rest of his guard have stopped as well, their eyes trained on the forest around us. "What is it?"

"We have company," he growls.

Aurick jogs up to our side, his teeth bared in a feral snarl as he keeps his gaze fixed on the woods. "A harpy," he says under his breath, and I watch as all the color drains from Engrid's face as she sits atop his back. His nostrils flare. "I scent only one," he adds.

"One is enough," Henrick replies darkly.

Another guard moves up beside us. Henrick turns to him. "Oryn, take the females. Run as fast as you can. Do not look back, and do not stop until you make it to the castle."

Henrick shifts back into human form so fast, I'm in his arms before I even realize what has happened. Gently, he sets my feet on the ground. "You must ride with Oryn, while I—"

"No," I state firmly. "I'm not going to leave you."

CHAPTER 21

HENRICK

"No," she refuses. "I'm not going to leave you."

I do not have time to argue with her. Before she can say anything else, I motion for two more of my guards to come to my side. "Take the queen and Engrid. Whatever happens, get them to the castle. Do you understand?"

They both nod.

"I won't leave you, Henrick."

Frustration burns through me. I turn back to her, ready to lift her onto Oryn's back, but I halt when she stretches up onto her toes, wraps her arms around my neck, and presses her mouth to mine.

Her lips are warm and softer than I imagined. She tastes of cloud berries and the first hint of snow. All rational thought leaves my mind as she traces her tongue along the seam of my mouth, asking for entrance.

I open my mouth and her tongue finds mine, curling

JESSICA GRAYSON & ARIA WINTER

around it and deepening our kiss. Unable to stop myself, I pull her close; completely lost in sensation.

Aurick clears his throat, snapping me back to the present. I force myself to pull away from her. Panting heavily, I drop my forehead gently against hers and stare deep into her hazel eyes as she whispers. "Please, be careful."

I'm still so stunned that I barely manage a nod. As her gaze holds mine, a strange warmth builds in my chest— something I have never felt before. "I will."

"Promise me you'll return to me."

I understand better than most that vows such as these are difficult to keep. "I cannot promise you this; anything is possible. But I vow to do whatever I must to return. My priority is to always remain at your side, my queen, and when I am forced to leave for whatever reason, I will endeavor to return to you quickly."

I cup her cheek. "You must go. Now. Before it is too late."

Dark laughter echoes from nearby. I grip Anna's forearm, pulling her behind me as I search the forest for my enemy.

"It *already* is too late," a woman's voice says darkly.

Movement in a nearby tree draws my attention and I look up to see the harpy. Obsidian eyes staring down at us from her perch.

As tall as one of my kin, her kind are almost as strong. But it is her wings that give her the advantage. I study her taloned feet, and worry trickles down my spine as I think of the damage they could do to my mate's soft and delicate flesh.

A low growl rumbles deep in my chest. "These forests around the castle are mine. Why are you here?"

She cocks her head to the side. Her white feathers ruffle in the cold wind as her dark red lips stretch into a sinister smile. "The Snow Queen sent me," she replies smoothly.

Ice fills my veins. "Why?"

"To see if it was true." Her gaze shifts to Anna. "She heard you had taken a queen. She wanted to know if her curse still bound your heart."

"Of course, it does," I growl. "She made certain of that when she encased it in ice." I bare my fangs in a snarl. "Leave now. While you still can."

Her dark eyes sweep over me and my men before she dips her chin in a mockery of a bow. "I will. And I will be sure to send your regards to my queen."

Without another word, she spreads her wings wide and takes off into the clouds, disappearing from view.

Panic tightens my chest. I don't understand why the Snow Queen wanted to know about Anna. I only know that she is dangerous, and I will do everything in my power to keep her from my bride.

I shift back into bear form and kneel before my queen. "Climb onto my back. Hurry," I add. "I want to reach the castle before nightfall."

Quickly, she climbs onto my back, settling between my shoulders.

I turn and address my guards. "Remain vigilant. We ride for the castle and we do not stop until we are safe inside the city walls."

CHAPTER 22

ANNA

As we continue onto the castle, I try to push away the terrible image of the harpy that has been burned into my mind. I'd heard they were terrifying creatures, but I'd never seen one up close before.

"Why do you think the Snow Queen wanted to confirm that you'd found a mate?"

"I do not know," he replies.

I wait for him to say something else, but he remains silent. He and his men are on high alert, constantly scanning our surroundings for danger.

So, even though I have more questions, I'm not going to ask them now. I'll wait until we're alone and safe in the city walls.

My mind keeps returning to Henrick's curse. The thought sparks a strange mixture of sadness and panic as I contemplate what else this may mean for him. We have not discussed it in great detail.

I wonder if it will shorten his life, or extend to his children. He said he didn't know how to break it, but the harpy's words suggest that it can be broken. After all, the Snow Queen sent her to see if his heart was still bound by her curse.

My thoughts turn to a report my father heard from a traveling bard several years ago. A princess in a neighboring kingdom had been cursed by a blood witch to sleep for eternity. No one knew how to break the spell.

I remember my parents warning us never to cross a blood witch. Their spells can be devastating and impossible to break.

We continue on in silence, and as the sun begins its slow descent on the horizon, I dig into my pockets for the dried meat I brought. "Want something to eat?" I ask Henrick.

"We should not stop," he tosses over his shoulder. He hesitates for a moment then adds, "But we can if you need to."

I smile at his thoughtfulness, but I've already learned how to eat while traveling. "Here." I lean forward and reach for his face.

He cranes his neck to examine my offering then takes it from me. "Thank you," he mumbles around a mouthful of food.

We continue in this way—one piece for me, another for him—until I've exhausted my supply. I'm full by now, but I doubt he is. Henrick is much larger than me, and I've seen how much he usually eats. "I'll bring more next time."

He looks at me. "Hopefully, there will be no need for long-term travel after we reach the castle."

When we reach the outer edge of the city, I'm surprised by how beautiful it is. A wall of white stone surrounds Kalysund, the capital of Arnafell. Covered in a fine layer of ice and topped with snow, it glistens beneath the last of the sun's rays.

Beyond the defensive wall, I can see the castle carved out of the mountain beyond. Built of white stone with veins of black and gray, it stands tall and proud. Square towers stretch toward the sky, the sharp-peaked, silver rooftops reflecting the soft glow of the lights of surrounding buildings.

The silver-and-blue banner of Henrick's House waves proudly from the tallest tower in the center. The forest falls away entirely; sharp lines of demarcation separate snow-covered fields from the dense woods.

A great horn announces our arrival when we approach the gates. The massive silver structures swing inward with a low groan as several bear-shifter guards pull them open, allowing us entry.

Flakes of snow twirl and dance on the breeze around us, lending enchantment to the city. It is both austere and yet beautiful.

"Your home is amazing, Henrick." The words escape my lips before I even finish the thought.

"It is your home now, too, Anna," he replies. "As queen of Arnafell, it is as much yours as it is mine."

His words touch me deeply, and tears spring to my eyes unbidden.

As we ride deeper into the city, people gather on either side of the main thoroughfare to greet us, watching with great interest.

I notice a mixture of Bear Shifters, humans, and the occasional Fae or Elf. My father's kingdom had little tolerance for anyone other than humans, but I am glad to see all are welcome in Arnafell.

The cobbled streets are perfectly kept, and the buildings

are well maintained. I notice the people appear well, also—no gaunt faces or thinly-dressed folk among them. Everyone seems to have what they need.

I suppose this makes sense, given how Henrick made sure to provide for his people in Islo and Kyruna. He is a fair and just king.

On our way, the sun drops below the horizon, and the city becomes lit with an ethereal glow. Lamp posts with radiant orbs of yellow light line the streets.

When we reach the castle, I notice the bear sigil carved into the silver doors, matching our banners. Behind the opening doors, people line the entryway to greet their king.

Henrick drops and allows me to slide off his back. He shifts then offers me his arm. Together, we walk into the castle, and he introduces me to the staff as their new queen.

This is such a stark contrast to my father's palace. All the servants there would hardly ever meet his gaze for fear of summoning his undue wrath. Henrick's staff greets him with a smile and friendly words.

The great entry room is sparsely furnished yet elegant. The floor is some sort of obsidian stone—a sharp contrast to the white stone walls scored by black-and-gray veins. Tapestries depicting great battles of Bear Shifters decorate the space.

Henrick guides me up a grand staircase in the back center wall leading to the next floor. At the top lies a grand balcony. I peek through the floor-to-ceiling glass separating us from the outside and note the lovely view of the city and the harbor just outside the wall.

Icebergs dot the ocean, and all ships appear to be docked.

Following the line of my attention, Henrick explains, "During the harder months, travel by sea is too treacherous for most. Many simply remain here until the warmer months melt the bergs."

I behold the line of ships with black sails, each bearing the bear sigil. "Is that your fleet?" He nods. "Why are the sails black instead of the colors of your house?"

A sly grin twists his lips. "Black sails are more formidable than blue, do you not agree?"

"Clever," I tell him. To intimidate any who would dare challenge him is wise, indeed.

He leads me down a long hallway lined with portraits of royals dressed in heavy robes and elegant dresses lined with fur trim. I assume these must be his ancestors.

When we reach the end of the hallway, he pushes open a great wooden door. My jaw drops as I step into the room.

A large four-poster bed stands along the far wall, the dark wood carved with images of snowflakes and bears. The mattress is piled high with white bedding and furs, warm and inviting.

My eyes are drawn to the fireplace next. The hearth is already lit with roaring flames, giving the room a cozy intimacy despite its spaciousness.

In the center of the floor is a sunken pool of water. A light mist of steam rises from the surface.

Henrick gestures to the pool. "There is a warm spring beneath the castle. We channel the water through the walls for our baths and plumbing." He gestures to a door in the right wall. "That is the cleansing room."

I turn toward the balcony on the opposite side of the bed. Made of floor-to-ceiling glass, the door slides open to the large balcony beyond, overlooking the city and the harbor. A table and chairs await us outside. Perhaps, when it is warmer, sitting on the balcony will be pleasant. For now, I'd prefer to stay indoors.

Large tapestries depicting winter scenes and castles cover the walls. The L-shaped sofa littered with plush white cushions provides a view of both the balcony and the fireplace.

Thick, white fur rugs are dispersed throughout the room, adding to the comfortable aura.

I turn to Henrick. "This is beautiful."

"These rooms are yours."

"Mine?" I frown. "I thought these were our rooms."

He shakes his head. "I do not need all this space. I prefer to give it to my queen." He pauses. "I will leave you to get settled."

Before I can respond, he leaves the room.

I sit on the sofa, staring at the hearth.

I thought Henrick and I would be sharing the same rooms, not living apart.

My parents have separate chambers because of my father's many infidelities. With Henrick, I thought it would be different. Part of me is relieved he doesn't expect me to share a marriage bed, but another imagines falling asleep in his arms every night and waking up with him each morning.

Honestly, last night at the inn was wonderful. I hoped we would continue in that manner, but it seems I was wrong.

I step onto the balcony, surveying the city and the ocean beyond. A cold wind carries the crisp, saline scent of the water, burning my lungs with each inhalation. I have never been so cold in my life, yet the pain slowly dulls and gives way to an invigorating thrill unlike anything I've experienced.

The city below me is blanketed in white. Smoke rises from the chimneys of the snow-covered rooftops. The orange glow of light from the many lampposts and homes lends the place a quaint, picturesque feel.

My new home is lovely in a way I never imagined. It may seem harsh outwardly, but I recognize the beauty at its very heart. Even the people are welcoming—something I never would have expected of Bear Shifters before meeting Henrick and coming to his kingdom.

Somehow, although we only met a few days ago, I'm already falling for my new husband. I never believed in love at first sight, and while this is not exactly first sight, it is certainly close.

I've known him for such a short time that the force of my feelings scares me. I always thought I would guard my heart closely before giving it away. However, Henrick's kind, thoughtful, and caring manner has stolen my heart little by little, each time he shows me what a good man he is.

Knowing that his curse means he cannot love me in return should be enough to dissuade the intense feelings I already have for him, but it is not.

I had a lot of time to think on our journey here, and I have come to a disturbing truth. I'm not just falling for him... I believe I have already fallen.

Sighing heavily, I step back into the bedroom, removing my clothes, discarding them on the floor next to the bed, and moving to the warm pool in the center of the room.

The water is wonderfully hot. As I sink into its depths, all the tension of the day leaves my muscles, and I release a soft sigh of contentment.

After I finish bathing, I dry off and slip beneath the furs in bed without dressing. Henrick's people are not bothered by nudity, and I'm too exhausted to change. I could call for Engrid, but I know she's had a long day, too, and I will not bother her for something so menial.

I turn onto my side and pull the furs over my shoulder, staring at the roaring fire in the hearth.

I know he cannot love, but is it possible, I wonder, for Henrick to feel even the smallest spark of what I feel for him too. I suppose only time will tell.

The harpy's words gave me hope, for they suggested that curse can be broken. If not, the Snow Queen would never have sent her to verify that Henrick's heart was still frozen.

CHAPTER 23

ANNA

A light knock on the door startles me awake. I rise from the bed and slip a robe over my shoulders, tying the sash loosely around my waist. Just because Henrick's people are all right with nudity, that does not mean I wish to parade around naked in front of them.

When I open the door, I'm greeted by a woman with white hair twisted atop her head in a tight bun and a kind face. Her bright blue eyes and towering height tell me she is a Bear Shifter like my husband. Although she appears human, she is far from it.

She bows. "Greetings, my queen. My name is Dalma. I've been sent by your husband to take your measurements for new clothes."

"Of course." I step aside for her to come in.

"I will make as many items as you like, but I will prioritize your coronation gown. King Henrick instructed that you are to be given whatever you desire. He simply stated I must make certain it is warm since humans do not do well in the cold temperatures like bears do. Your kind are fragile compared to ours."

Her words are blunt, but I understand she means no insult. She is simply stating a fact as she sees it. "Thank you."

I didn't realize I would attend a formal coronation ceremony, though that is standard for most royalty.

Dalma guides me to a small step stool in front of a large mirror, and I strip away my clothing so she can measure me.

At the sound of her gasp, my eyes snap up to hers. "What is it?"

"You are quite…" She clears her throat, failing to mask her concern. "You are smaller than I thought."

I frown. "Is that a problem?"

She shakes her head, but I note the strange hesitance in the movement.

"What is it?" I ask. "Tell me."

"It just… reminds me of the king's sister. She was small, as well."

"Henrick has a sister?"

"Had."

Henrick never mentioned that. "What happened to her?"

"She died several years ago. Fell to a plague that swept through Arnafell."

My heart clenches. "That's terrible."

"Aye, she was only a year younger than him. They were close. He and his older brother loved her very much. When she died, they were devastated. I believe that is why he sought out the Snow Queen when his brother fell ill. He could not stand to lose someone else."

"And that is how he became cursed," I murmur, more to myself than to her.

"Aurick told me that you knew," she says. "He also told me you are brave—a true Queen of the North."

My eyes snap to hers.

"Aurick is my son." She smiles proudly. "And I gather he is quite taken with your lady-in-waiting."

I smile. "I believe Engrid feels the same."

Dalma laughs softly. "I suppose time will tell." She glances her material and lifts a bolt of fine silken fabric. She arches a brow. "Would you like me to make you something... for the king's eyes only?"

Henrick and I have not joined yet, but the mere thought of being this intimate with him makes my entire body fill with warmth. I reach out and lightly trace my fingers over the soft material, imaging how it may feel against my skin. When I don't answer right away, she adds, "How about I make something, and then you can decide later on if you wish to wear it or not?"

"Yes," I tell her. "That would be good."

"Excellent," she replies. "I will make several, just in case any are ruined during your mating cycle."

Mating cycle? I open my mouth to ask, but she turns her attention to the light-blue silk fabric and begins measuring. "King Henrick is a good and just ruler. That is why we are so overjoyed he has finally married." She smiles. "When he returned from Solwyck after Princess Halla rejected him, we all grieved for our king. He is a good man—always looking out for the people."

Despite knowing this all happened before he met me, I cannot help the sharp stab of jealousy tearing through my heart at the reminder that I was not his first choice.

If Princess Halla had accepted him, he would have chosen her instead. Everyone knows of Princess Halla and how she slayed a dragon, saving her people and the kingdom of Solwyck.

They say she is as beautiful as she is brave. There were rumors she would never walk again, after the injuries she sustained from the battle, but, last I heard, she had regained some use of her legs.

I don't get a chance to ask Dalma more before another knock on the door demands my attention. I pull a robe over my shoulders and call out, "Enter!"

Aurick and Engrid enter a moment later. She approaches me, smiling brightly. "My rooms are next to yours, and they have a lovely view of the water."

I'm glad she's so close to me. In my father's castle, all the servants lived in the basement.

Aurick sweeps into a bow. "I see you have met my mother."

"Yes." I smile. "She is lovely."

Dalma and Aurick grin at the compliment.

"The king has requested your presence in the throne room," he says. "I will lead you there."

I glance at Dalma. "I have all the measurements I need," she assures me. "I will return in a few days with your new clothing. Do not worry, Your Majesty. It will all be ready in time for your coronation."

Engrid darts a glance at Aurick. "Will you please wait outside while I dress the queen?"

As soon as they're gone, I turn to Engrid. She is not just my lady-in-waiting; I consider her a friend—a good one. In her role at my father's castle, she was always privy to secrets passed among the staff. She often found out about a new mistress before my mother did. I know she hated giving my mother such news, but Mother appreciated knowing in advance rather than getting caught off guard when Father moved a new woman into his chambers.

"Engrid, I need you to do something for me."

"What is it?"

"As you're settling in here, can you see what you can find out about the... joining habits of bear-shifters?"

"Joining habits?" She blinks in confusion, before her

mouth drops open in astonishment. "Surely you do not suspect the king of—"

She stops short, but I know she is thinking of my parent's situation, so I quickly reassure her. "No, not that. I just… Dalma mentioned something about a mating cycle, and I would like to know what that entails."

She smiles, obviously relieved to hear I do not suspect my new husband of acting like my father. "Of course, my queen. I will let you know what I find out."

CHAPTER 24

ANNA

Engrid helps me into a long, light-blue dress tunic with silver threads, trimmed with white fur around the collar, bell sleeves, and hem. She braids my long, chestnut hair so it hangs to one side over my shoulder. As I admire myself in the mirror, I tip my chin up. "How do I look?"

She smiles. "Like a queen."

Aurick leads me down the hallway and staircase to the throne room. It's hard not to gape as I enter. The floor space is huge, and the tall ceilings make it even grander. Sunlight spills in from the windows, casting sparkling patterns across the tile floor.

At the far end, there are two thrones. Henrick is seated atop one carved of black stone, and the one beside him is white. He stands as I walk toward him and extends his hand toward me.

I take it, and he squeezes gently, gesturing to the white

throne. "This is yours, Anna. I wanted to show you the throne room and palace before your coronation ceremony."

"Thank you, Henrick."

I take a seat on the throne, resting my arms on the armrests and surveying the room. I shift in my seat because it's stiff and uncomfortable, but I don't suppose I'll be seated here very often.

Henrick frowns. "Would you prefer a cushion?"

"It's fine, for now. I think I can manage for a few hours."

"Yes, but what about the entire day?"

I blink. "The coronation ceremony lasts that long?"

"No. We will be here together each day."

My heart stops. "You… want me ruling with you every day?"

"Of course, I do," he answers as though my question were ridiculous. "You are the queen. My co-ruler."

"I…" I'm not sure what to say. I hardly expected he would consider me more than a queen in name only. I certainly did not believe he intended for me to rule beside him.

He cocks his head to the side. "This displeases you?"

"No. I—I just did not think you would want me to rule alongside you." I stumble over my words. "My father certainly did not give my mother the honor."

He frowns. "I am not your father. I married you because I wanted someone to share my rule, not a figurehead." He lowers his gaze. "But if you do not wish to—"

I take his hand, rushing to answer, "I do." His eyes flash to mine. "I want to share our rule, Henrick. It's just… not something I expected you to want, as well."

A faint smile tilts his lips. "You are good and kind, Anna. You are also clever and brave. I suspect you will make a fine ruler for Arnafell."

A slow smile curves my mouth at his praise. "Thank you, Henrick."

"Now"—he gestures to the white throne—"would you like a cushion?"

Gently, I squeeze his hand. "Yes, I would."

As he goes over what will happen during my coronation, I pay close attention so I'll know what to expect.

"There will be visiting dignitaries from a few of the neighboring kingdoms," he says. "They will mostly be allies, but some merely want to remain on good terms with Arnafell."

His words give me pause as I think of Princess Halla. "What about Solwyck? Will anyone come from there?"

"Yes. Princess Halla and Prince Errik will come in place of her brother, King Gerold."

I scrutinize his face but see nothing to suggest any hard feelings. Still, despite my better judgment, I must ask. "Princess Halla... you approached her to marry you."

I let the unspoken question hang in the air between us.

"Yes," Henrick replies. "I did. They will arrive tomorrow."

He continues discussing the ceremony as though I have not just brought up a woman who rejected his hand. She is either a raw subject for him, or he simply does not care—his expression is impassive, so I cannot tell which.

When he's finished walking me through all the steps, he holds out his hand and smiles at me. "I have something I wish to show you."

His grin is so handsome, I cannot help but smile in return when I rest my palm in his. "What is it?"

"Come," he says, pulling me toward a door behind the thrones. It blends so well into the wall that I didn't see it until now. He takes my hand, resting it on the wall. Gently, he pushes forward, and the door swings in on hidden hinges.

Bright light filters in, and we step through into the most enchanting space I've ever seen. My spirits lift as I take in the courtyard in the center of the castle. He leads me down a gravel path toward a large fountain in the middle. The water is frozen in a cascading pattern from the tallest level.

"In the warmer months, the water will begin flowing again. But these"—he gestures to the roses all around us —"bloom all year long."

Thick bushes full of crimson-and-white roses are planted everywhere, the delicate fragrance mixing with the crisp saline breeze from the ocean just beyond the city walls. Vines full of vibrant, blue flowers climb the walls all around us.

"This is beautiful," I murmur. "But how is this possible?"

"This space was enchanted long ago by the High Elves of Rivenyl as a gift to one of my ancestors. The very air is charged with life. Anything can grow in this space without tending."

He guides me past the fountain on a winding path to another hidden door in the wall. "This connects to your room. You simply have to take the stairs; they will lead to an opening near the bed."

"But… I saw no door there."

"You wouldn't." He grins. "It is concealed and only accessible if you know exactly how to find it. Come, I will show you."

He guides me up a spiral staircase, and sure enough, we reach a door at the top. He carefully pushes it open then steps into my bedroom.

My gaze drifts to the bed, piled high with soft furs. The roaring fire in the hearth warms the space, but as I study my husband, I recognize that it is not the true reason my entire body flushes with warmth.

Henrick shows me the hidden panel along the wall to

access the door. He's right; if he hadn't shown me, I would never have found it.

He leads me onto the balcony. Together, we stand at the railing, gazing out at the city below and the sea beyond.

"Is it not too treacherous for Princess Halla to travel by sea?" I ask. Solwyck, her kingdom, lies across the narrow strait.

Henrick nods. "It is dangerous, but not for Halla and Errik."

I frown. "Why is that?"

"Errik is one of the Merfolk. His people can help guide their ship around any potentially dangerous icebergs."

"Her husband is Mer?"

"Yes, but he can shift forms and walk on two legs when out of water."

I've never heard of a shifting Mer. I open my mouth to ask another question, but he interrupts. "Would you like a tour of the city?"

My ears perk up. "Yes, I would."

"Come then, my queen. Let me show you part of your kingdom."

I smile as he leads me across the hallway, down the grand staircase, and out the castle doors.

CHAPTER 25

ANNA

I expected a carriage ride through the city, but Henrick takes us on foot instead. With my arm looped through his, we make our way down the main thoroughfare with Aurick and a few of the guards trailing behind.

He takes me down a road lined with various shops, some peddling clothing and others jewelry and wares. The thick scent of spice and cooked meat drifts on the wind, and my stomach begins to grumble loudly.

Henrick turns to me. "Would you care to eat?" He gestures to a nearby restaurant.

I glance inside the window to see the space filled with customers seated at long rows of tables. Servers move back and forth, bringing plates of food and drinks to the customers. Warm steam rises from the mugs, suggesting they may be drinking tea or some other deliciously warm beverage to combat the chill in their bones.

"Yes, I'd love to."

The moment we enter, all heads turn to us, and one of the

servers rushes forward. She bows low. "My king." Her gaze shifts to me, her blue eyes glowing brightly. "My queen. What an honor it is to receive you. Please"—she gestures to a nearby table—"have a seat."

As soon as we sit down, the server passes us bowls of thick stew. It smells so delicious, I can hardly wait to try it.

"Warm tea or heavy cider?" The server asks me. Her gaze drops to my abdomen, and I understand what she is asking— I shouldn't be drinking if there's a chance I'm with child.

Even though I'm sure it will fuel rumors that I'm already carrying the king's child, I've always preferred tea, so that is what I order.

All eyes turn to me when the customers hear her confirm my drink order. My cheeks heat under the scrutiny, but when I glance at Henrick, he is already eating his stew.

I decide to follow his lead. He doesn't care about gossip, so I'll do the same. I dip my spoon into my bowl and bring it to my nose. The stew smells so delicious. I take a bite, and a delightfully spiced flavor rolls across my tongue. "This is wonderful," I murmur.

"We can have some sent to the castle whenever you'd like," Henrick offers.

"That sounds lovely."

The stew is so tasty, I eat another bowl after Henrick's encouragement to have all I want. I heard most men prefer their wives to not eat too much for worry that they'll gain weight and lose their figures. Henrick, it seems, does not have this concern.

When we are finished, he takes me to a nearby jeweler. When we walk inside, the owner greets us warmly. "My king! My queen! It is good to see you both. Come"—the old man ushers us in invitingly—"see what I have done."

I frown, uncertain what he's referring to. I don't get a chance to ask before he leads us to the back of his shop, where a delicate, silver-ringlet crown sits on a plush cushion. "What is—"

"Your crown," Henrick says. "As queen, you choose the jewel that will rest in its setting."

"Oh." I didn't know this was a tradition. "What are my choices?"

The owner signals toward a cabinet full of sparkling gems of all different sizes, each more beautiful than the next.

A giant ruby and an emerald capture my attention first, but it's a small, sparkling, ice-blue stone that draws me in the most. I motion to the gem. "What is that one?"

The color reminds me of Henrick's ice-blue eyes. Perhaps that's why I am so interested.

The jeweler frowns. "Oh, that is a simple winter stone, my queen. It is much smaller than the others and the least valuable."

Henrick turns to me. "Each of these stones is from the royal treasury. You may choose any you wish. I requested they be displayed for you to decide."

I nod and turn my attention back to the gems. The small, ice-blue one calls to me, and I do not care if it is less valuable than the others. It's the one I want. "I choose that one."

The jeweler looks to Henrick for guidance, shocked that I would want what he obviously considers an inferior stone. Henrick simply nods, and the man removes it from the casing.

"Of course, my queen. It will be ready in time for your coronation."

"Thank you."

CHAPTER 26

HENRICK

The day passes by quickly. By the time we return to the castle, the sun is already low on the horizon. We eat dinner, then I escort Anna back to her rooms.

When we reach them, she turns to me. "Would you like to come in for some tea?"

A smirk twists my lips as I recall her ordering tea in the restaurant. "You will only create more rumors if you insist upon tea instead of cider."

She laughs. "So, you caught that, too? And here I thought you were not paying attention."

"I am always paying attention." I cup her chin and tip her face up to me, looking into her lovely eyes. "Especially when it comes to you."

Her cheeks flush a lovely shade of pink, and she lowers her gaze. She turns away, retreating into her bedroom and sitting on the sofa by the fire. I take the seat beside her.

"Did you enjoy the day?"

"Very much." She smiles. "The city is lovely. The people are friendly and… all of this"—she scans the space—"feels like a dream."

I tilt my head to the side. "That is a good thing?"

"Yes, it is."

The light of the fire frames her features in a warm glow, lending her an ethereal countenance. I study her hazel eyes, noticing the small flecks of green in her irises. Anna is the most beautiful female I have ever seen, and I can hardly believe that she is mine.

I am curious about something, however. "The winter stone," I begin. "Why did you choose it?"

It is the one I favored as well, but I desire to understand why she did. Just as I long to know everything about her.

Her gaze holds mine as she slowly reaches out to touch my face, and whispers softly. "It reminds me of your eyes."

My eyes travel to her full, perfect, pink lips as I remember our kiss. I wonder if they are as soft as I remember.

A few long tendrils of hair have escaped her lovely braid to frame her face. I reach out and gently tuck them behind her ears. Her gaze holds mine as I cup her chin, brushing the pad of my thumb over the petal-soft flesh of her cheek.

A pink bloom spreads across her face and the bridge of her nose as her eyes stare deep into mine. I lean forward and gently brush my lips against hers.

She inhales sharply, and I pull back. "Forgive me," I murmur. "I—"

I do not get to finish because she presses her lips to mine, silencing me abruptly. They are warm and even softer than I remembered. She traces her tongue along the seam of my mouth, and when I open, her tongue curls around mine, deepening our kiss.

I am lost in sensation as I stroke my tongue against hers, longing to stroke my *stav* deep into her channel.

She moans lightly into my mouth, and my stav hardens and extends with the desire to join our bodies. I gather her into my arms and pull her into my lap.

She comes willingly without breaking our kiss and settles over me.

CHAPTER 27

ANNA

His eyes are heated. The light of the fire casts his face in harsh relief, his square masculine jaw and brow appearing even more severe than usual. However, I know it is nothing more than a mask that hides who he truly is.

I reach up, tracing my fingers lightly across his brow, smoothing out the crease of his perpetual frown. His ice-blue eyes study me intently as I move down farther and cup his cheek.

I run the pad of my thumb across his lower lip, remembering how soft they were against mine.

His nostrils flare. "Anna." His voice is a low growl, heat flaring in his gaze.

I lean in and press my lips gently to his again.

He gasps, and I curl my tongue around his. He returns my kiss with an urgency that steals the breath from my lungs.

Without breaking our kiss, he lifts me into his arms and carries me across the room. He lays me in bed and moves over me, kissing me until I'm panting and breathless beneath him.

He pulls back, his eyes searching mine. "Anna," he growls, and it is easy to see that he is struggling to maintain his control. "Are you certain you want this?

I love that he asks instead of simply taking. I reach for his cheek. "Can we just kiss and touch for now?"

He groans with desire. "I will take anything you will give me, my queen."

I reach up and unfasten the clasps of his tunic, sliding the fabric off his shoulders. My fingers trace the hard planes of muscle lining his abdomen and chest. He pulls back just enough to meet my gaze entreatingly, and I'm struck by how fierce and beautiful he is—like a marble statue of masculine perfection made manifest before me.

He searches my face for a moment before I reach up and cup the back of his neck, pulling his lips back to mine. I guide his hand to my breast and gasp as he brushes his thumb over the peak. I arch into him. He growls in response and slices a line down the fabric covering me.

It falls away from my body, leaving me bare beneath him. When he pulls back, his gaze travels over me like a gentle caress. "You are perfect," he whispers. "More beautiful than anything I have ever seen."

I open my mouth to speak, but he crushes his lips to mine, branding me with the fire of his kiss.

He rips his mouth away to press a series of kisses along my jaw and down my neck then closes his mouth over my breast, laving his tongue across the sensitive peak. I thread my fingers through his hair, holding him in place. Need pulses through me as he begins a gentle suction that has my back bowing.

"Henrick, please," I whisper, though I'm not even sure what I'm asking for.

He turns his attention to my other breast then moves down my body. When he reaches my mons, he lifts his head. "I want to taste you, Anna. Will you allow it?"

Breathless with anticipation, I barely manage to nod.

He fists the silken scrap of material between my thighs and rips it from my body. When he drags his tongue through my already slick folds, I nearly come undone, then he reaches the small bundle of nerves at the top.

I've touched myself before, but it's never felt like this.

A low moan escapes me as he teases his tongue over the softly hooded flesh. I dig my heels into his shoulders and back as my hips rise to meet him.

He growls, and the vibration shoots through me, setting every nerve ending on fire with his touch.

When he begins a gentle suction, my body goes taut like a bowstring. Suddenly, I'm coming harder than I have in my life. I cry out his name as wave after wave of pleasure floods me.

He continues teasing his tongue through my folds, wringing out every last bit of my orgasm until I'm completely spent.

He presses a tender kiss to the inside of my thigh and moves up my body, capturing my mouth with his. When he pulls back, he gently brushes the hair back from my face.

His ice-blue eyes delve into mine as I reach up and touch his cheek. With another kiss, this one more tender than the last, he rolls onto his side, pulling me with him while tucked against his chest.

I snuggle into his embrace. His length is a hard bar between us. "You are still—"

"My needs can wait," he murmurs, placing two fingers under my chin, "until you are ready to fully mate."

After a while, he moves to stand. My grip tightens, and he stills. "What is wrong?"

"You're not going to stay?"

He frowns. "Do you wish me to?"

I take his hand in mine. "I… thought we would share our chambers since we are married."

He blinks. "You want me to remain here with you? Always?"

My cheeks heat under his scrutiny as I nod. "Yes."

A handsome smile curves his mouth. "Then I will stay."

He pulls me even closer to his chest, cradling me. The steady rhythm of his heart against my ear makes me feel safe. I love lying wrapped in his arms.

He smooths his hand up and down my back as we drift off to sleep.

I breathe deep of his masculine scent and determination fills me anew. I am already in love with this man. And I will do whatever it takes to break the curse, and melt the ice around his heart.

CHAPTER 28

HENRICK

Anna stirs gently in my arms as the first rays of sunlight spill in from the balcony. I enjoy sleeping close to her. Leaning forward, I gently nuzzle her hair, drawing in a deep breath of her delicate scent into my lungs as I commit it to memory.

As I study my beautiful mate, a sharp pain stabs in my chest, followed by a slight, dull ache. I press a hand to the space directly over my heart. Perhaps it is the ice—the curse fighting to remain in place as I fall under Anna's thrall.

She is mine, and today she will be crowned queen of Arnafell before our people. I am beyond happy she has expressed she likes it here.

I am eager for her to meet Halla, too. She is a kind person, and I am certain she and Anna will get along rather well.

Gently, I brush the hair back from Anna's face and whisper in her ear, "It is time to wake up, my queen. You must get ready for your coronation."

Her eyelids flutter open, and she gives me a sleepy smile,

nestling against me. "I'm not sure I want to leave this bed. It's warm here."

"I can shift into bear form and keep you warm."

"That would be a sight, wouldn't it?" She laughs. "To be snuggled against you during the ceremony."

"If you wish it, it shall be done," I tell her. "You are queen, and I would see that your every desire is met."

She beams then presses her lips to mine.

"Halla and Errik should be arriving soon."

Her face falls. "Oh." I'm about to ask what is wrong when she smiles faintly and adds, "That sounds wonderful."

Her expression suggests otherwise.

Perhaps she is nervous to meet new people. Once they arrive, I'm sure Halla and Errik will put her at ease with their friendly and open manner.

A gentle knock at the door begs my attention, and I move to open it, finding the seamstress, Dalma, on the other side.

She greets me with a warm smile. "It is good to see you, my king."

"You, as well."

Her arms are laden with many items, as are her assistant's behind her.

I move to the side, allowing them to enter, and Anna jerks upright in bed, eyes wide. "Henrick, I'm not clothed."

Guilt floods me. "Forgive me, I—"

Dalma and her assistant frown and retreat to the door, but Anna stops them. "Wait!" she calls out. "It's all right. I... suppose I'd have to be undressed for this anyway, right?"

Dalma bows low. "Yes, my queen."

Anna stands, wrapping the sheet around her as she moves to a dressing stool Dalma places before our large mirror.

The first things Dalma gives her are undergarments: a scrap of material to cover her pelvic area, and a strap that covers her breasts.

Desire burns through me. My need for her is still great, so I force myself to turn away so she can change.

I wait for a few minutes, pretending to gaze out the balcony window to the city, then turn back around. When I do, I swallow thickly, my eyes rapt with awe.

The silk hides nothing of her beautiful form from me— the sensuous curve of her breasts or the gentle flare of her hips. My stav lengthens and extends, urging me to join my body to hers, but I force myself to push these thoughts aside.

Anna is not yet ready to fully mate, and I will respect her wishes.

My thoughts drift to the way she responded to my touch. Not long ago, she expressed she may never invite me to her bed. I am pleased that she has changed her mind.

I have many duties to attend to, but I cannot force myself to leave Anna just yet. I am transfixed as Dalma and her assistant dress her in their various creations.

When she dons her coronation dress, my mouth drifts open involuntarily. She wears a long, flowing, ice-blue gown with clear gemstones sewn into the fabric along the bodice and down the length of the skirt. The style accentuates the elegant curve of her neck and her slim shoulders. Her long, chestnut hair is tied in an intricate braid over her left shoulder.

She turns to me, shining with happiness. "What do you think?"

"It is as though you are dressed in pure starlight."

Her smile brightens.

A light knock on the door signals another servant: the jeweler with her crown. He hands it to me, and I see the gemstone is a perfect match to her ice-blue dress. I scrutinize the stone, remembering why she picked this one above all the more valuable choices.

As if sensing my thoughts, she joins me, gently tracing her

fingers across the stone. "It's beautiful," she whispers. "And the exact same color as your eyes."

When she lifts her gaze to mine, a strange ache grows in my chest. The dull ache around my heart becoming stronger a moment before settling. She is so breathtakingly beautiful. I am almost afraid to touch her, for she is surely too perfect to be real.

Her lips curve into a stunning smile. "What are you thinking, Henrick?"

My eyes memorize every contour and line of her face. "A great many things, my queen."

How was I ever so blessed to be bound to someone so perfect?

CHAPTER 29

ANNA

Only a few hours before our ceremony, I notice a ship approaching the harbor. The banner proudly displays a bright, golden sun. I recognize the banner of Solwyck. Dread settles deep in my gut; this must be Princess Halla and Prince Errik.

Henrick waits patiently for them to arrive while my body is a bundle of nervous energy practically bouncing off my throne. Glancing over at him, I wonder if he is excited, or if he dreads seeing the woman who rejected him so recently.

As I study him, I cannot tell, and it frustrates me to no end.

I shouldn't care that he once wanted her.

At least, that's what I keep trying to tell myself. Yet I cannot stop thinking about it.

The doors to the throne room swing open, and one of the guards announces Princess Halla and her husband.

My lips part. Halla is stunningly gorgeous. With crimson

hair, bright-blue eyes, and a small dusting of freckles across the bridge of her nose and cheeks, she is lovely to behold.

I notice her steps are slow and a bit awkward. It seems she has not fully recovered from her injury when she slayed the dragon that attacked their kingdom, but, at least, she is able to walk.

She holds onto her husband's arm, and I shift my attention to him. I'm surprised by how human Prince Errik appears even though he is Mer. As he moves closer, I note the fine layer of scales across his body, so close to human skin that only a glint of light reveals the pattern. His ears, I note, are tipped like an Elf or Fae, and his eyes glow a deep, ocean-blue color.

Halla beams at Henrick, stepping forward to hug him. Jealousy churns deep in my gut like bitter acid, but I force my face to remain neutral. She moves to me and does the same.

Errik shakes Henrick's hand, then mine.

"I'm impressed you traveled by ship," Henrick says. "It is a dangerous endeavor this time of year."

Errik smiles. "We have the help of my people to guide us around icebergs. The distance across the strait is so short we thought of swimming it, but"—he places his palm over Halla's lower abdomen—"we did not think it wise for Halla to swim in cold water with me because of our child."

Henrick smiles. "You are expecting. This is good news."

Errik wraps a possessive arm around Halla and presses a tender kiss to her temple. "Yes, we are thrilled."

Halla comments, "Gerold is excited, as well. He can hardly wait to be an uncle."

"I imagine he is," Henrick adds, and I wonder exactly how close he was to her family before Halla rejected him.

As much as I want to dislike Halla or find fault with her, I cannot. She is a lovely person, as is her husband. Her bubbling laughter is contagious, and I find myself just as fascinated with her stories as my husband seems to be.

When they excuse themselves to dress for the ceremony, Henrick turns a sharp gaze to me, studying me intently. He rises from his throne and takes my hand, pulling me up beside him. "Come with me."

I am perplexed but follow him anyway. He leads me behind the thrones to the secret doorway to the rose garden.

It's cool outside, but not unbearably so. As soon as we pass the door, he seals it shut behind us and spins to face me. "You do not need to be jealous of Halla."

My mouth drifts open. I could deny it, but I want nothing but honesty between us. "I was, but not any—"

He seals his mouth over mine, cutting off my sentence abruptly. His tongue invades my mouth, curling around mine and stealing the breath from my lungs.

My heart pounds against my ribs as he pulls me so close there is no space between our bodies, lips repeatedly meshing with mine. "Can you not see"—he breathes between kisses—"you are the only one I want?"

Desire pulses through me as he dips his hand beneath the neckline of my dress and cups my breast. I moan into his mouth as he brushes his thumb across the sensitive peak.

"I have thought of nothing but your smiles, your lips, and the taste of you on my tongue all day, Anna," he whispers against my lips. "You are the most beautiful female I have ever seen."

He moves down my body and closes his mouth over my breast, laving his tongue over the beading tip. His hands sink and grip the hemline of my dress. He pulls it toward my hip, and his fingers trace over my thigh.

I gasp when he pulls the lace between my thighs to one side and drags his fingers through my already slick folds.

When he reaches the small bundle of nerves at the top, a low moan bursts free.

He captures my mouth in a searing kiss, swallowing all the small sounds of pleasure I make while continuing to run his fingers through my folds.

He pulls back to lock his ice-blue eyes onto mine then carefully inserts one finger into my core. My lips part on a breath as he adds another and begins to gently pump in and out, his thumb teasing over the small pearl of flesh at the top.

"I want to watch you find your pleasure," he growls.

Every muscle in my body locks up, then I'm coming harder than I ever have before, crying out his name as I find my release.

As I come down from my orgasm, he removes his fingers and brings them to his mouth, closing his lips over them. His eyes roll to the back of his head as if I'm the best thing he's ever tasted.

He captures my mouth in a claiming kiss then drops his forehead to mine. "Never doubt that I desire you above all else in this world, Anna."

I wrap my arms around his neck and embrace my heart's desire as I whisper in his ear, "I love you, Henrick."

When he does not say it back, I still for a moment, before I remember that he cannot. Then he presses his lips to mine and kisses all my uncertainty away.

Even if his heart remains frozen, surely my love can be enough for us both.

CHAPTER 30

HENRICK

The throne room is bursting with people—dignitaries and citizens of Arnafell who have come to see their queen's coronation. As I sit on my throne, waiting for her to enter, my mind keeps returning to the words she spoke in the garden: *I love you, Henrick.*

My heart squeezes painfully in my chest, just as it did at that moment. No matter how desperately I wish I could say it in return, I cannot. The curse prevents me; my heart remains frozen.

And yet, I have never felt this way about another before. If the feelings I have for Anna are not love, surely they are close.

The crowd hushes as my wife steps inside and slowly approaches the dais. Once she stands before me, I take her hand, guiding her to the white throne beside mine. Her luminous eyes pin me as I place the crown atop her head. I glance at the blue gemstone she chose because it reminded her of my eyes.

She is perfect, my Anna. Even if my heart is unable to love her, I will care for her, protect her, defend her, and devote my life to her until I draw my last breath.

And I will do these things, not just because she is my mate, and it is the way of the North and of my people... but, because she is everything to me.

CHAPTER 31

ANNA

The celebratory feast for my crowning is a jovial event. Minstrels play lively music as couples whirl across the floor.

Aurick approaches and whispers something in Henrick's ear. Henrick nods, and I watch as Aurick moves to Engrid's side then offers her his hand. She accepts, and he leads her to dance in the center of the room, surrounded by a few other couples.

Henrick turns to me. "Would you like to dance?"

"Yes, I would."

He stands and takes my hand, guiding me toward the other dancers. As soon as he finds an opening, he wraps an arm around my waist and pulls me onto the floor.

I'm not entirely familiar with this form of dance, and I misstep, nearly sending us both tumbling. He catches us before we fall and eyes me curiously. "Do you not know the *trulca?*"

"Um… no, I don't." I feel eyes boring into my back.

Nervously, I tuck a stray tendril of hair behind my ear. "I... suppose I should learn for next time."

I start for my seat, but his hand is still in mine. Gently, he tugs me back to him. His eyes study me for a moment. "I have an idea."

"What?"

"Stand on my feet."

"I—won't that hurt you?"

He arches a brow. "I am a Bear Shifter. I am very strong, my human queen."

I laugh. "All right, my strong bear-shifter king." I step up onto his feet and grin. "Lead on."

He begins to dance. We whirl and spin around the other couples as I cling to him.

Henrick smiles at me, twirling us around, and I cannot help but smile in return. I'm breathless in the best way. I haven't had this much fun in... I cannot even remember how long.

A few locks of hair escape my braid again, floating around my face. Henrick gently reaches out and brushes them back into place between songs.

As we dance, everything else falls away, his ice-blue eyes capturing mine. We laugh as we spin across the floor, keeping time with the music.

When the band winds down, Henrick offers me a glass of wine. I'm not normally one to drink since I've seen what it does to my father, but I don't see another option. "No water?"

Henrick glances back at the table and shakes his head. "I can ask the servants to—"

"That's all right," I tell him. "I don't need it. Wine will be fine, for now."

I put the cup to my lips and take a sip. The taste of berries and sunshine rolls across my tongue. I've never tasted such a delicious wine. I down it and hold the glass up to Henrick. "Where is this from?"

"Islo," he says. "It is winterberry wine. They harvest the berries and make the wine during the warmer months."

I watch as Princess Halla and Prince Errik take a turn about the floor. Their dancing consists of Errik lifting Halla into his arms and holding her to his chest. She wraps her arms around his neck as he dances for them both.

For a Merman, he certainly moves elegantly on two legs.

When the music dies, they return to our side. Errik and Henrick step away for a private chat, and Halla joins me. She smiles. "I'm glad Henrick found you. He seems… very different than when I met him in Solwyck."

I frown. "Different how?"

"Lighter. Happier," she replies. Her gaze darts to her husband. "Like a man in love." She laughs softly. "In fact, I do not think I even saw him smile or laugh even once when he came to visit us."

This surprises me, but also makes me feel warm inside. I love thinking that I may be the cause of his smiling and laughter.

My thoughts turn back to my confession.

I told him I love him, but he did not say it back. He cannot because of his curse. However, perhaps the words do not need to be spoken. After all, is it not obvious in the way he cares for me and regards me as his queen and mate?

"He helped me save Errik, you know."

My eyes snap to hers. "He did?"

"Yes. Errik was injured, and I needed the help of a blood witch to heal him. Henrick took me to her when I was unable to walk. He warned me not to make a deal with her for Errik's life, but I didn't have a choice."

As she tells me the story of how Henrick helped her, I think back on the Snow Queen—the blood witch who cursed

Henrick. I want to ask him more about it, but I do not know how much he will tell me.

There has to be something more to it, that might help us figure out how to break his curse.

When the night winds down, guests begin to trickle out. Halla and Errik bid us goodnight and follow a staff member to their guest rooms.

I'm so tired, I can barely keep my eyes open.

Henrick touches my cheek. "All you all right?"

"Yes. Just sleepy."

He dips his chin. "I'll take you to bed."

Although I know he means he's taking me back to our rooms, part of me hopes he means something else entirely. He places one arm behind my back and the other under my knees, lifting me to his chest.

I wrap my arms around his neck and lean against his heavily muscled body as he carries me up the stairs. Inhaling deeply, I breathe in his masculine scent. "You always smell so good," I murmur.

He dips his head to my collarbone, and a pulse of heat shoots through me at the low growl in my ear. "So do you."

I'm surprised when Engrid greets us as we enter the room. She helps me out of my clothes and into a nightdress, little more than a slip of fabric hanging down to my mid-thighs and held up by two thin straps.

I recognize the material. This is one of the garments Dalma made "for the king's eyes only."

When Engrid leaves, I emerge from behind the changing screen, and Henrick's eyes flare with heat.

Gently, he tucks me beneath the covers and crawls in beside me. The fire is blazing in the hearth, warming the entire room. Snow falls gently outside, reminding me how cold it is beyond the windows.

As I snuggle against Henricks warmth, he wraps his arms

around me, holding me close and covering us both with another blanket and a layer of furs.

With my back pressed to his chest, his stav is a hard bar against my backside. A rumble rises from his chest as he nuzzles my hair then presses a line of kisses along the curve of my neck.

I reach back, running my fingers through his hair before turning my head to face him. He captures my lips in a claiming kiss and cups my breast with one hand, my mons with another.

My body lights on fire beneath his touch, and I moan into his mouth as he pulls the fabric of my gown up and lightly drags his fingers through my slick folds.

He doesn't take long to bring me to completion. I cry out his name as I find my release.

Turning onto my back, my gaze travels down his body. His stav is still erect. A bead of liquid forms on the end, and I lift my eyes to his and stroke his cheek. "I want you, Henrick."

His eyes search mine. "You are certain?"

"Yes. I love you, Henrick."

Sadness flashes across his face at my words. Again, he remains silent. My heart sinks. I swallow against the knot in my throat, studying his reaction to what I will say next. "Do you... feel anything... close to that, Henrick?"

He lowers his gaze. "I... am uncertain."

His words hit me like a physical blow, robbing the breath from my lungs. Tears sting my eyes and blur my vision, but I blink them back. I know he is cursed, but I'd held onto the small hope that he might feel something. Emotions lodge in my throat, and I cannot speak around them.

He pulls me to his chest and runs a hand over my hair. "I'm sorry, Anna," he whispers against the shell of my ear. "I wish so badly that I could. But I cannot." He pauses. "I can promise you loyalty and devotion, but love is something I may never give to you. Not because I do not wish to, but because my heart is frozen and it cannot be thawed."

"Are you certain of that?" I ask.

His brow furrows deeply. "It is my curse."

"Yes, but… if it cannot be broken, why would the Snow Queen send the harpy to see if it was still in place?" I cup his cheek. "Don't you see? If she was so worried that she sent someone to verify it was still in place, that means she was concerned that her curse was failing."

My mouth drifts open as I consider her words.

She continues. "Perhaps the ice around your heart is already melting, Henrick. The way you've treated me… if that is not love, I don't know what is."

As much as want to believe it's true, I also do not want to embrace false hope, only to have that hope ripped away from me later. "The way I treat you, is the way any Bear Shifter would treat his mate. It does not mean my curse is lifting."

CHAPTER 32

HENRICK

She looks devastated.

"But the way you've held me, taken care of me… saved me, even. Why would you do these things if not out of love?"

"You are my mate," I declare. "It is my duty to protect and care for you, Anna."

She lowers her gaze. "Your duty," she murmurs. "Of course."

"I am sorry, Anna. Truly."

When I bring one hand to her face, her hazel eyes snap up to mine. "Why did I only find out about it because of Aurick. When were *you* going to tell me?"

"I wanted to tell you on our wedding night. I meant to pull you aside and speak to you before we said the words of our bond, but I could not bring myself to for fear you'd reject me. And I could not let you go. Not after I realized who you were."

"What do you mean, *who* I was?

I cup her chin. "You are the woman I have seen in my dreams these past few years. You are my fated one."

"What are you talking about?"

I turn onto my side and gently run my hand from her shoulder down her arm to her hand, threading my fingers through hers and bringing our joined hands to my chest. "My people believe we are given dreams of our fated one. Some of us are blessed enough to find them in this life, but others are not.

"When I saw you, I knew it was truth. You are *her*. The woman I have dreamed of for years. You are a gift from the old gods. You are my fated mate."

"You should have told me," she says bitterly. "You should have warned me before—"

"Before what?"

"Before I started to fall in love with you, Henrick." Her eyes flash with anger before sadness and devastation steal over her features. Tears escape her lashes and roll gently down her cheeks. "What if we have children?" her voice quavers. "Will you be able to love them?"

"I cannot love, Anna. I would protect and defend our children from all harm. I would raise them in the ways of both your people and mine. I would—"

"Give them everything but the love of a father," she blurts, finishing my sentence in a way I would not have.

She is right. Guilt tears at my heart. "Forgive me, Anna. I should have told you sooner."

She sits up in bed, pulling one of the furs around her naked form. "Yes, you should have," she snaps. "If you had, I would have been more careful to guard my heart."

"Please, Anna. I'm sorry. Please, forgive me."

"I know not every marriage is blessed with love, Henrick. But how can I subject a child to a life without it?" Another tear slips down her cheek. "My father did not love me or my brother. We were only ever bargaining pieces to him. That's why he gave me to you. I always hoped to marry for love, because I didn't want to raise a child the way I was raised."

I reach out and gently brush the tears off her face with my thumb. "Forgive me, Anna. I..." I pause, unsure whether I want to say the words. I offered them once, but I am hesitant to offer them again. I cannot bear the thought of losing her, and I know that once they are spoken, they cannot be taken back. "I will release you from our bond if that is what you want."

She lowers her gaze and shifts away on the bed. "I... I cannot give you an answer right now. I must think on it."

A deep ache settles in my chest at her words—pain so powerful it robs me of the ability to speak. I somehow manage to nod.

I watch her roll onto her side with her back to me. I reach for her, but she pulls away. "Don't. Please. I... cannot be close to you now that I know... you feel nothing for me."

It isn't true. I do feel something for her, but I do not understand it. It is more than just wanting to protect her because she is my mate. I want to please her and coax smiles and laughter from her lips. Not because it is my duty, but because it gives me joy to know that she is happy.

But I cannot tell her this. I will not give her false hope when I am not even sure what it is that I am feeling. I retract my hand silently.

She turns to regard me. "I'm sorry, Henrick. It's just too painful right now. I... need some time. Maybe with time, I can—" Her voice hitches.

Another tear escapes her lashes and rolls down her cheek. As much as I want to reach for her, I force myself to remain still. She does not want my touch anymore.

She turns her back to me again, and I listen as she struggles to hold back her sobs before finally drifting off to sleep.

CHAPTER 33

ANNA

A week has passed since Henrick told me his curse remains unbroken. I'd hoped that perhaps our bonding might have started to melt the ice around his heart, but I was wrong.

It's so hard to be around him when everything he does makes me feel so loved. It only makes it more painful when I remember that he cannot truly love me despite the fact that he goes out of his way to be thoughtful. And each time he insists I remain at his side in the throne room, discussing matters of state with traveling dignitaries and the defense of the kingdom with his guards.

He includes me in every decision of the workings of his kingdom. He truly considers me his co-ruler and queen. I do not know many kings who would share such power with their wives, and I consider myself truly blessed to have found one who does.

Each day we spend together, I find myself falling more in love with Henrick, despite my attempts not to. When he smiles at me, my heart breaks because I know he can never return these feelings. They will be forever unrequited—he will never love me as I do him. All my joy has turned to ash, and my heart is devastated beyond measure.

When I return to my chambers after dinner, I step onto the balcony. The cool wind whips through my hair and tears at my body. I wrap my fur coat ever tighter around me to ward off the chill.

A noise behind me draws my attention. "Are you well?" Henrick's voice filters in from the bedroom.

"Yes."

He moves behind me. Slipping his arms around my waist, he pulls me back against his chest and gently nuzzles my hair. When he acts like this, my heart flutters in my chest. Just as it does when I see his handsome smile.

A lone tear escapes my lashes and rolls down my cheek.

He stills then turns me in his arms to face him. He cups my chin, tipping my face up as he brushes away the tear with his thumb. "You are upset. Why?"

Because I am in love with a man who will never love me in return.

My heart hurts every time I remember that he will never know love again.

I open my mouth to speak, but a subtle knock at the door interrupts me.

"Enter," Henrick calls.

Aurick steps inside and drops his head. "My king, Prince Malak is here to see you."

"Is he alone?"

"No, he travels with his pack, but they have come unarmed."

A frisson of worry ripples down my spine. I've heard Wolf Shifters can be aggressive and dangerous, but Henrick said he and Malak used to be as close as brothers. "Do you believe he might try to harm us?"

"Never," Henrick says, his voice full of conviction. "Come. I will introduce you to him, and we will see what he has traveled to visit us."

Henrick offers me his arm, and I loop mine through. Together, we make our way to the throne room. My heart once again squeezes painfully in my chest at his actions. He includes me in all matters because I am his queen.

If only he could love me, too.

CHAPTER 34

HENRICK

I t has been many years since Malak came to my court. He used to visit each season, and we would spend our days hunting the forests and racing across the great ice plains.

His eyes widen slightly as I introduce Anna. He steps forward and bows before her. "It is an honor to meet you, Queen Anna."

She smiles at him. "Henrick says you are his friend. You may call me Anna."

His gaze shifts to me, and I recognize the question in his eyes. We were once more than friends; we were like brothers. But now… things are strained between us ever since Malak's brother took the throne.

He dips his chin. "And you may call me Malak, Anna."

Something about her smile, at him, stirs my possessive instincts. A warning growl issues from my chest, and Malak blinks in surprise before a grin curves his mouth. "I have not come to steal your mate from you, Henrick."

I narrow my eyes at his teasing. He knows as well as I do that possessive instincts for one's mate run strong in shifter males. "Why, then, have you come?"

"Have you heard of the cursed Dragon of Eryadon who lives by the sea?"

"Yes, I have."

"Did you hear that his curse has been broken?"

"Yes, I had heard this." I lean forward. "What does this have to do with anything?"

"I would think *you* would be very interested in this." Malak arches a brow. "The Dragon's curse has been broken, and he is now happily mated to a human. He was cursed by a blood witch as well."

My lips part at the realization, and I stand from my throne. "If he can break a curse set upon him by a blood witch, then—"

"Your curse may be broken, also," Anna finishes my sentence.

Hope shines in her eyes when they meet mine. I curl my hands into fists at my side, determination bolstering me. I will do whatever I must to break my curse. Anna deserves a male who loves her, and I want to be that male.

Halla and Errik will leave in a few hours. And Errik is the person who first told me about the dragon's curse being broken. The Dragon of Eryadon is the one who gave Errik the blue pearl that allows him to walk on two legs so he may live with his beloved on dry land.

I invite Malak to dine with us before they leave, wanting to find out everything he, Errik, and Halla know about how the Dragon broke his curse.

Errik studies me. "You seem changed since I last saw you.

Not as… remote and cold." He pauses. "Are you certain the ice around your heart is not already thawing with Anna at your side?"

In truth, I have wondered the same, although I always come to the same conclusion. "I do not know."

"The Dragon's curse could only be broken if his true love looked upon him. What are the terms for breaking yours?"

Malak looks to me and frowns. "There weren't any that I can remember."

"You were there with Henrick?" Errik asks Malak.

"He was," I explain. "He accompanied me to the Snow Queen's kingdom. Malak and I grew up together." I look to Anna, remorse filling me at the decision I made long ago. "He tried to talk me out of it, but I insisted. I was desperate to save my older brother."

With a heavy sigh, Malak shakes his head. "I'd hope to convince you not to do it."

"It is not your fault that I did not listen, my friend."

Errik turns his sharp gaze to me. "I understand what it is to care for someone that much that you will do anything to try to save them."

Halla turns to Anna. "I have seen the way you two look at each other. It is the same way Errik and I do." Her gaze flicks to me. "Are you certain that the ice around your heart is not already beginning to thaw?"

"In truth, I do not know," I answer, and I hate the sadness in Anna's eyes as she gazes at me. I long only to make her happy.

"What will you do?" Errik asks.

"The only thing I can—I will travel to the kingdom of the Snow Queen and ask her to end my curse."

"No, you will not," Anna says. "It's too dangerous. I won't let you go."

"I would go for *you*, my Queen," I remind her. I have to. I want to make Anna happy; I want her to stay with me. Always.

Her eyes shine with a strange mixture of sadness and anger. An uncomfortable silence settles around the table before she clears her throat. "We will speak of this later."

I dip my chin. "Later, then."

CHAPTER 35

ANNA

I am sad to see Halla and Errik leave. They were good company, and I now count them among my friends. However, I am glad that Malak is here, for there are things I must ask him. I want to know every detail of what happened when Henrick went to the Snow Queen. I want to know exactly how dangerous she is, and the likelihood of my husband returning to me alive after he seeks her out again.

Henrick and I argued almost as soon as Halla and Errik left. He insists upon going to the Snow Queen despite my begging him not to.

Frustrated and not wanting to argue any longer, I told him I needed some time to myself. I also need to find Malak and speak with him.

It does not take long to find Malak wandering the palace grounds. He strolls around the main courtyard, which looks nothing like the secret garden behind the thrones. Everything here is ice, snow, and thick vines bare of leaves. A menagerie of stone and ice carvings decorate the space—

images of bears dressed in full battle armor and other creatures such as Dragons, Fae, and Mer. Curiously, Malak is
studying the only statue *not* depicting an otherworldly
creature.

Carved from white marble, the human woman is lovely to
behold. Elegant lines and delicate features suggest she is
fragile, but the expression on her face speaks of fierce determination that would challenge any who would dare think
her weak.

"Malak." I call his name gently.

He turns to me, blinking several times as though coming
back to himself. "Yes, Anna?"

I could try to ease him into this conversation, but I am
queen of the North, and if I have learned anything from
Henrick, it is that blunt truth is valued here above all else.
"How dangerous is the Snow Queen?"

"Very," he replies. "She is a formidable foe." He steps
closer, his glowing green eyes grave. "Henrick is fortunate
she did not kill him or turn him into one of her ice statues
when he first went to see her."

"Why did she let him live?"

"She fell in love with him. I suspect her curse was created
as much out of sadness as it was anger. I imagine it would
have been difficult for her to keep a statue of him in her
castle." He pauses. "So, instead, she cursed him so that if he
could not love her, she wanted him to love no one at all."

"Were they"—I hesitate, unsure if I want to know but also
realizing I need an answer—"in love?"

He shakes his head. "Bear Shifters mate for life. That is
why Henrick could not lie to her and bed her as she'd asked
him."

"If she's so dangerous, why have you come here to
convince him to break his curse?"

"Because he is my friend, and I would have him returned

to the person he once was. And I had heard that he found a mate."

His gaze turns longingly once more to the statue of the human woman. "I know what it is to love someone you cannot have. I would not see someone else suffer this fate. Does it not bother you that he cannot return your love without breaking his curse?"

"It does, but not enough to encourage him to visit someone as dangerous as the Snow Queen. I love him, and I would not see him place his life in danger," I finally answer. "All those years ago, why didn't you stop him before he made a deal with her?"

Tensing, he turns his attention toward the castle with a faraway look as if reliving the memory. "He would not listen to reason." His hands curl into fists at his side. "I should have tried to kill her rather than let her make a deal with him."

"My queen," Engrid calls. I turn to find her walking toward me. "The king was searching for you. He wanted to know if you were ready to have dinner."

"Yes, I'm ready." I glance back at Malak. "Would you like to join us?"

"Of course."

CHAPTER 36

HENRICK

At dinner, I am glad to see Anna has so readily accepted Malak into our circle, just as she did Halla and Errik.

Aurick rushes into the dining hall, interrupting us. His eyes wide in concern.

"What is wrong?"

"Forgive me, my King, but we have received word from the North."

"What is it?"

"The Snow Queen is marching toward Arnafell. She has attacked our border, near the city of Kyruna."

Anna gasps and turns to me, eyes wide with concern. She fears for the people of Kyruna, as do I.

"Why would she attack now?" I look between Malak and Aurick. "After all these years since I crossed her?"

Anna turns to me. "The Snow Queen asked for you heart, but you refused, so she cursed you. She sent the harpy to

189

ensure her curse was still in place. Maybe the harpy told her something that—"

"Malak eyes snap to mine. "Anna is right. The Snow Queen made an example of you—the powerful Bear King of the North. If she believes her curse may be waning, it would make her appear weak. She cannot tolerate that. Not if she wishes to keep control of her power and her lands. Her entire reign is built upon fear. So now she must prove her power by defeating you. She is worried your marriage to Anna will break her curse. That has to be why she would attack now."

Henrick's gaze snaps to me. "Then, perhaps my curse truly can be broken without her."

"If it can, and if she defeats you before the ice around your heart has melted, no one will ever know that her powers failed," Anna adds.

"What will you do?" Malak asks.

"We will meet her forces at the border and push them back."

Malak straightens. "I will return to Winterhold, and ask my brother to send you aid. Surely, he will do this, knowing that if Arnafell falls, Winterhold would be next."

I dip my chin. "Thank you, my friend."

I face Aurick. "Inform the men. We leave at dawn."

CHAPTER 37

HENRICK

Anna is silent for the rest of our meal. When we retire to our chambers for the evening, she says nothing, crawling into bed with her back to me as she has done every night since I told her about my curse.

So, I'm surprised when she turns and folds herself into my arms. "Don't go," she whispers against my chest.

"I must."

"Can you not send your forces instead?"

"What kind of king sends his men into a battle where he will not go himself?"

"My father, for one."

I sigh heavily, taking advantage of her proximity to pull her closer, running my fingers through her long, silken hair. "I am a different kind of king, then."

"I know," she murmurs against my chest.

"If all goes well, I can break my curse and—"

She rears back. "Is that why you insist on going?"

I cannot lie to her. "Partly, yes. But I would lead my men in battle, too."

"We may be able to break the curse without her help, Henrick. Even if we cannot, I don't care about the curse anymore."

I frown as I recall the distance she has kept from me every night since she found out, and the sadness in her eyes each time she looks at me. "I thought you—"

"I was foolish." Her voice quavers. Tears brighten her eyes. "You are a good man. Even though you cannot love me, you care for me, protect me… you are always thinking of me and my comfort. If that is not love, I do not know what is. I love you, Henrick. You say you cannot return those feelings, but it doesn't matter. What we have between us, is close enough, my love."

"I must do this, Anna. Even if there were no curse, I must defend the kingdom. I have to go."

Her grip tightens. "Stay with me."

"I cannot."

Her hazel eyes meet mine, full of determination. "Then take me with you."

My heart squeezes painfully in my chest.

She truly does love me, and I do not deserve her love.… not when I can never match it.

"No. It is too dangerous."

"I don't care. I'm going with you."

"No, Anna."

"I'm *going*."

"I have granted you everything you could possibly want, but this, I will not give you." I caress her cheek. "You are too important to me. I will not allow you to step into harm's way."

She says nothing, but in her eyes, I read her determination. She will not be easily dissuaded from this path. So, instead, I will placate her and slip away before she wakes in the morning. It is the only way to be sure she remains behind where she is safe.

"Now, I understand why Malak made the choice that he did," I murmur into her hair.

"What do you mean?"

"He gave up someone he cared for… and he did it to keep her safe."

"She was human too, wasn't she?"

"How did you know?"

"I saw him staring at the ice carving of a human woman in the gardens." She lifts her gaze to mine. "Was it a likeness of her?"

I nod. "Her name was Luna. Malak loved her, but his family did not approve of the match *because* she was human. They threatened to harm her. So, he sent her away for her safety."

Anna meets my eyes evenly. "I won't leave your side. I will not allow you to face the Snow Queen alone, Henrick."

I brush a stray tendril of hair behind her ear and hold her gaze. "Let us discuss this in the morning. Rest, Anna." When she nods, I pull her back to my chest, smoothing my hand down her back. "Tomorrow may be a very long day."

I hate deceiving her, but I have no choice. She is stubborn, my mate, and I can think of no other way to make certain she stays here.

She closes her eyes, and I listen to the soft, even sound of her breathing as she falls asleep.

When I wake in the morning, the sun has not yet risen. I make my way to Aurick's chambers. I have a request I know will be difficult for him to grant.

He opens the door, staring at me in astonishment. "My king, what is—"

"I need you to remain here when we march."

He frowns. "But my king, I—"

"I want you to stay with Anna. If I should fall, I can think of no one I would trust to guard her better than you."

He drops into a low bow. "You honor me, but I would see you safely through battle, Henrick." He uses my given name as he did when we were children.

I shake my head. "*She* is more important."

Reluctantly, Aurick dips his chin. "Understood, my king."

CHAPTER 38

ANNA

When I wake, the fire is still burning brightly in the hearth, but Henrick is not in bed. Light spills in through the balcony window, and I jerk upright when I realize just how late it must be.

I do not have time to call Engrid to help me dress, so instead, I dress quickly in a tunic and pants. I ordered them made so riding on Henrick's back would be much easier when we travel.

As soon as I'm clothed, I race out into the hallway and down the stairs. I find Aurick in the great entry room. "Where is—"

"He left, my queen."

"*What?* When?"

"Early this morning. He did not want to wake you."

I bluster. "He didn't want—"

This was his plan all along.

He never intended to take me with him.

Anger floods my system, and I glare fiercely at Aurick. "Take me to him."

"I cannot, my queen. He ordered me to protect you."

I draw in a deep, steadying breath as I struggle to control my fury. "Then to obey your king, you will have to escort me to him, or else risk his wrath when he finds out I followed him alone."

Aurick blinks at me, mouth agape. "My queen, you cannot—"

"I can, and I will. Now take me to the king."

He runs a hand roughly through his short, dark hair. "As you wish, my queen."

CHAPTER 39

HENRICK

Upon arrival in Kyruna, I can hardly believe the devastation before me. Smoke rises from the charred rubble of destroyed buildings. The silver metal of the great city gates appears to have suffered damage from a battering ram, but the gates are intact.

As we approach, they slowly open inward, and several people rush to greet us, including the Mayor. "My king, we are glad to see you," she says. "We held the city, but just barely."

I survey the damage. "I can see that. We are here to defend and push back the invasion."

"Come," she says, leading me up the stairs of the wall that surrounds the city. She points into the distance. "They came from that direction. They attack each morning at sunrise. Yesterday, they gave us an ultimatum: Surrender at dawn, or they will kill every man, woman, and child in Kyruna."

"And the Snow Queen? Does she march with her army?"

"She does, my king."

I must find a way to reach the Snow Queen. *I have to—*

"My king! A rider approaches from the south!"

I rush toward the southern part of the wall, near the entrance to the city we passed only moments ago.

"Who is—" I stop when I recognize Aurick. I run a hand roughly across my stubbled chin at the realization that Anna rides on his back.

I race down to the gates, anger pulsing through my veins like liquid fire. I left her behind for good reason. How dare she come here and put herself in danger?

The gates begin to swing open as I boil with rage.

I can't believe—

All thoughts leave my mind, along with the ability to form words, when she slides off Aurick's back and rushes into my arms.

She crushes her lips to mine in a searing kiss, and I'm completely lost.

When she pulls back, instead of softness in her eyes, I see nothing but unbridled anger. "How dare you leave me behind, Henrick?" she snaps. "You knew I wanted to come with you. I —" Her tirade cuts off when she notices spectators watching us intently. She clears her throat then turns to the Mayor. "Do you have somewhere the two of us may confer alone?"

"Yes, my queen. This way."

Anna takes my hand, and we follow the Mayor. Despite her attempt to exude a calm demeanor, fire smolders in Anna's eyes.

We are led to the same inn we stayed in before—one of the few buildings that did not sustain damage. When we enter the room, it is just as we left it. A warm fire lights the hearth, and the bedding is piled high with furs. I can hardly tell a war is waging just outside the city wall.

Anna turns to me, her eyes full of betrayal and fury. She

opens her mouth to speak, but I capture her lips in a searing kiss.

At first, she tenses, but then she melts in my embrace. Clutching me, she curls her tongue around mine, deepening our kiss.

"Oh, Henrick," she breathes between kisses. "You left me, and I was afraid I might never see you again."

I taste the warm salt of her tears with each press of her mouth to mine. I'm so happy to hold her in my arms, kissing each tear from her cheeks. "Do you not know I would do anything to keep you safe, Anna?"

"I would do the same for you, Henrick." She takes my hand and pulls it to her chest, directly over her beating heart. "I am your queen and your mate. That means whatever may happen, we will face it together, my love."

My love.

The words fill my heart with joy. Not long ago, she did not even want me to touch her.

I drop my gaze to our joined hands and squeeze hers gently. "You truly love me, even if I cannot—"

She presses a finger to my lips to silence me. "It doesn't matter." She stretches onto her toes and brushes her mouth against mine. "You already have my heart. It is no longer mine, Henrick. It belongs to you."

Pure happiness blooms in my chest. I lift her into my arms and carry her to the bed. Gently, I lay her beneath the furs and crawl in beside her. I trace my hands over her body as her tongue curls around mine.

She arches into my touch and moans softly into my mouth as I carefully undress her, leaving her bare beneath me. I pull back to admire her bare form. Her long hair is spread out beneath her, and her hazel eyes are intense.

"You are beautiful, my Anna."

She curls her hand around the nape of my neck and pulls my lips back down to hers.

I kiss a heated trail down the elegant column of her neck, tasting the sweet salt of her skin until I reach her breast. I close my mouth over the peak and lave my tongue across the tender flesh until it beads beneath my attentions.

I move to the other breast as she threads her fingers through my hair. She is panting and breathless beneath me while I kiss a line farther down her body.

She tightens her grip on my scalp as I reach her folds, and I lift my head to look at her. Gently, she pulls me back up until my face is level with hers.

I search her eyes. "Are you certain you want me?"

"Yes, Henrick," she breathes. "I do."

CHAPTER 40

ANNA

Henrick watches me with a hungry gaze as I trace my fingers over the hard planes of muscle lining his chest and abdomen. When I reach his *stav*, I wrap my hand around his length. He is so big my fingers do not quite touch.

A bead of liquid forms on the end. He swipes his thumb over the tip and then trails it over my lower abdomen, marking me with his scent. "Tell me you are my mate," he growls.

I cup his cheek. "I'm yours, Henrick."

I part my thighs so he can settle between them. The crown of his stav bumps my entrance, and I inhale sharply.

Bracing his weight on his elbows on either side of me, he palms my cheek. His ice-blue eyes never leave mine, and the breath stutters from my lungs as he slowly enters me.

At first, everything is tight and uncomfortable. A tear slips down my cheek as he breaks through my barrier, and he stills.

"Are you all right?" he whispers, brows drawn together.

"I just need a moment," I breathe as tight heat blooms inside me.

He brushes my tear away with the pad of his thumb then presses a gentle kiss to my lips as my body slowly adjusts to his invasion.

I wrap my legs around his hips, and he begins a slow and steady rhythm, moving deep in my core.

The exquisite friction of his stav is unlike anything I've ever felt. I trace my fingers over the strong muscles of his back, feeling them flex beneath my hands with each stroke of his body into mine.

"Henrick," I whisper. "More."

He increases his pace. The small muscles of my channel begin to flex and accommodate his length. "So tight," he rasps, barely maintaining his control.

His ice-blue gaze holds mine, and a deep growl sounds in his chest as each stroke becomes deeper and stronger, bringing me close to the edge of my release.

My toes curl with pleasure as he leans in and devours me with a kiss, his powerful body moving over mine and claiming me with each thrust.

"You are mine," he growls. "My queen, my mate. My Anna."

"Yours," I barely manage to gasp through my pleasure.

He lowers himself so his chest and abdomen are flush with mine, wrapping his arms around my back. His eyes are fiery and possessive, and the vibration of his growl shoots through me, tipping me over the edge.

I cry out his name, finding my release while wave after wave of pleasure moves through me.

My release triggers his. "Mine!" he roars above me, his stav pulsing deep in my core as he erupts inside me, filling me with the delicious warmth of his seed.

After what feels like forever, he's still hard inside me. He reaches down and brushes the damp hair back from my face, studying me like I'm a rare and precious treasure. He leans down and captures my mouth in a claiming kiss. "You are my mate, Anna."

"And you are mine, Henrick," I whisper against his lips.

Still sheathed deep inside me, he rolls us onto our sides. He holds me to his chest so tenderly I melt against him as he combs his hands through my hair, gently nuzzling my temple.

CHAPTER 41

HENRICK

When I wake in the morning, the first of the sun's rays are just barely peeking above the horizon. The light filters in through the window, casting a warm glow throughout the space.

Anna is still asleep in my arms. She is so beautiful, it hurts. My heart squeezes painfully in my chest, and the dull ache settles in like it always does when I am with her, as if her mere presence is chipping away at the ice frozen around my heart.

Perhaps that is what this pain has been all along—a slow erosion of the Snow Queen's curse.

Gently, she stirs in my arms. Her eyelids flutter open, and she gives me a sleepy smile. I press a peck to her lips.

A light knock on the door interrupts us, and I call, "Who is it?"

"Aurick, my king. The Snow Queen's army is approaching. She is riding at the front and has sent a messenger asking to speak with you."

Anna bolts upright. "What will you do?"

"I must speak with her. If there is any way to avoid further casualties or damage to our side, I must try."

She strokes her thumb across my cheek. "But Malak said she is dangerous."

I meet her gaze evenly. "So am I."

CHAPTER 42

ANNA

Henrick stands just inside the gates, waiting for them to open. He turns to me and places a knife in my hand. "Keep this on you at all times."

I tuck it into my boot for easy access, then stretch onto my toes and wrap my arms around his neck. I brush my lips against his in a tender kiss, and he bows his forehead to gently touch mine.

"Please come back to me."

"I will do everything I can to return to your side, Anna. You have my word."

The gates open. He pulls back to take both my hands in his and presses a tender kiss to the back of my knuckles then turns to leave.

It takes all my control not to rush after him. I hate letting him go.

I watch on the wall as Henrick goes to meet the Snow Queen. She is not at all what I expected. With long, silver-white hair, her skin is pale as snow, and her lips are tinted blue instead of red. She is beautiful in a haunting way. She is clothed in a white dress covered in crystal-like flakes of snow, and her crown appears to be made of solid, finely sculpted ice.

She narrows her eyes. "So, the rumors are true. You have taken a queen."

They are close enough I can hear every word they speak.

"Yes," he replies.

"I want to meet her."

"No," he snarls. "She stays on the wall."

"If you want to broker peace, I must meet with the queen, as well."

His protest cuts off when he whirls to find me striding through the gates. I move to his side and tilt my head to proudly meet the Snow Queen.

I am Queen of the North. I will not show her my fear.

Her eyes are striking and calculating—white irises with a thin rim of ice blue around the edges.

I take Henrick's hand in mine, squeezing gently. Whatever happens, we will face it together.

Her gaze drops to our joined hands, and she arches a thinly sculpted brow. "You are in love with him, even though he is incapable of loving you in return."

"Yes," I declare. "I am."

She turns her attention back to Henrick. "Do you realize how rare such a creature is? To love knowing she will never be loved in return?" She narrows her eyes at me. "That is... if it indeed true and not merely infatuation."

She reaches out to touch my face, but I jerk away from her icy grasp.

Henrick snarls, "You wanted to speak. So, we are here to broker peace between our two kingdoms."

She cackles. "Oh, you think I wanted to discuss terms for peace? No. I simply wanted to see you again. But this"—she gestures to me—"is a surprise. A very good one, at that." He bares his teeth in a feral snarl, and she levels an icy glare at him. "Give her to me. I desire her presence in my court. If you do this, I will withdraw my army, and there will be peace between us once more."

"Never," he roars. "You cannot have her."

"Then I will take you instead." She touches his other hand, and I gasp when ice begins to form across his skin.

It spreads quickly down his torso and legs, freezing him in place. When the ice reaches his neck, his panicked blue eyes meet mine. I scream at the sight of him turning into a perfect frozen statue.

"No!"

On the wall, Henrick's men and the people of Kyruna wail and roar in anger.

Tears sting my eyes. "What have you done to him?"

A smirk twists her lips. "I have frozen your king. Your kingdom is mine. I am the new ruler of Arnafell."

"Turn him back. *Now!*"

She laughs. "No. I will not. He will make a fine addition to my court."

Blinding anger floods my veins, and with a swift movement, I pull the knife from my boot and lunge at her.

She ducks to one side. Lightning fast, she grips my wrist and twists the blade in my hand. Turning it back on me, she plunges it deep into my side.

I stumble back as her ice-cold gaze holds mine.

Aurick roars, and in the corner of my vision, I see him leading Henrick's men toward us.

The queen throws out her hand, erecting a wall of ice between us and halting their advance. Aurick pounds and scrapes against the frozen barrier. Fissures spread across the wall like fine webbing as the Bear Shifters struggle to break through.

She leans down and studies me with sick fascination etched in her features. Pain blooms across my torso and blood pools on the ground beneath me. "Did you truly love him?"

"With all that I am," I grind out.

"How interesting." She flashes a menacing grin. "I shall consider him one of my finest pieces. Do not worry. He will always have a place in my court, where he can keep me company for all of eternity, trapped in his icy form."

My heart stutters and stops. "He's not dead?"

She laughs. "No, of course not. Merely frozen."

I glance at Henrick, determination steeling my nerves. I will not allow her to imprison my beloved mate. I grip the knife handle and rip it from my body.

The Snow Queen only has an instant to gape at me before I sink the blade deep into her chest.

She falls to one side, gasping for air. Her gaze fixes on the sky overhead. "Clever… human," she chokes out before her eyes close and she stills.

CHAPTER 43

ANNA

A sharp *crack* slices the air, and the ice wall crumbles away as Aurick and his men break through. I press my hand to my side to stem some of the bleeding and twist my body toward Henrick.

I reach for him, and a pained smile curves my mouth as the ice cracks around his body and falls away. In an instant, Henrick is thawed and awake.

His eyes are wide as he turns to me. He drops to his knees and gathers me into his arms. "Anna, hold on." He places his hand where the knife pierced my flesh. "I'm going to get you help." He lifts his head and cries out, "The queen needs a Healer!"

Darkness begins to close in around the edges of my vision. I'm vaguely aware of a flurry of activity all around me that I can only hope is a Healer working to help me somehow.

CHAPTER 44

HENRICK

Blood blooms across her torso, the rush of scarlet overwhelming me with fear. Anna stares up at me, her face unnaturally pale.

"Anna, please," I beg as tears sting my eyes. "Hold on. The Healer is coming."

A sharp pain stabs at my chest, stealing the breath from my lungs. My heart pounds as heat builds deep within me. Emotions lodge in my throat as the ice melts from my heart.

The Snow Queen is gone, and so is her curse.

Pain and devastation fill me as I cup Anna's cheek. "I love you, Anna." The words leave my mouth, driven by conviction. "You are my heart. You cannot die, my beloved queen."

A tear slips down her cheek. "I love you too, Henrick."

"Anna, I—"

I choke as her eyes close, and she goes limp in my arms. Only the shallow rise and fall of her chest tells me she is still alive.

The Healer falls to her knees beside Anna.

"Please," I gasp. "You must save her."

"I will do what I can, my king," she vows.

CHAPTER 45

ANNA

Heat is the first thing I am conscious of. I inhale deeply and detect the masculine scent of my husband. I shift, and his strong arm tightens around my waist, pulling me back into his chest.

Memories slowly return, and I realize I no longer feel pain. I place my hand to my side, where my wound was, and feel only the outline of a scar. Carefully, I turn in Henrick's arms to face him and find his ice-blue eyes already open.

He cups my face and presses a tender kiss to my forehead. "Thank the gods you're awake." He hugs me tightly to his chest. "I love you so much, Anna. I was so worried."

I pull back to search his face. "You love me?"

A devastatingly handsome smile curves his mouth. "The Snow Queen's curse melted away when you killed her." He grows serious. "I love you, Anna. You are my heart."

Joy brighter than a thousand stars fills me. I throw my arms around his neck and press my lips to his. He claims my mouth in a searing kiss, stealing the breath from my lungs.

"I love you," he whispers again between each press of his lips as his hands dip beneath the hem of my gown and trace over my already sensitive skin.

In one swift movement, he rolls me beneath him. His hips press insistently against mine. He tunnels his fingers into my hair, angling my face to his as he devours me with his lips and his tongue.

"I'm yours, Henrick," I whisper against his lips.

Without hesitation, he extends sharp claws and slices my nightdress away from my body. He runs his hands down my frame, leaving a trail of fire on my skin, in their wake.

His nostrils flare as he moves over me. "I can scent your need, my mate."

I open myself to him, and he notches his crown at my entrance.

His gaze holds mine and a low moan escapes my parted lips as he slowly enters me.

Henrick groans when I wrap my legs around him. "You're so tight, Anna," he grits through his teeth. He begins a slow and steady rhythm, and I arch to meet each movement of his body over mine, the delicious friction of his stav causing pleasure to coil tightly in my core.

"You are mine," he whispers. "My beautiful queen, and my mate. I love you, Anna."

"I'm yours, Henrick," I moan, sensation overwhelming me with each thrust of his hips into mine.

When I come, it's with a keening cry. He roars above me. His stav begins to pulse as he releases deep inside me, filling me with his seed.

I haven't even recovered from my orgasm when he begins anew, his erect stav making long strokes into my channel. "I need you again, Anna."

I wrap my arms and legs around him, holding him close

as he thrusts into my body. This time, we come together. I'm panting breathlessly beneath him as he reaches down to touch my face. His gaze holds mine, shining with devotion.

"I love you, Anna. With all that I am."

"I love you too, Henrick. My fierce Bear King."

EPILOGUE

ANNA

As I stroll through the secret courtyard, surrounded by the beautiful, enchanted roses, awareness prickles my flesh.

I freeze before warm arms slip around me from behind. Henrick pulls me back against the solid warmth of his chest. He tenderly nuzzles my ear as he splays his open palm over my lower abdomen.

I place my hand over his and squeeze gently. "I came as soon as I heard you were searching for me. Is everything all right, my Anna?"

I turn in his arms, stretching onto my toes until my face is almost level with his. Gently, he drops his forehead to mine. "I just came from the Healer."

Worry flits across his expression. "Is everything all right with our cub?"

"Our cubs are fine."

His brow furrows. "Cubs? As in... more than one?"

I beam and nod. "Twins."

He crushes his lips to mine as he lifts me into his arms.

He pulls back just enough to pepper kisses across my cheeks, brow, and nose. He lowers my feet to the ground and drops to his knees. Placing his hands on either side of my waist, he presses a tender kiss to my belly.

I thread my fingers through his hair, and he lifts his gaze to me, his eyes bright with tears.

"Does this make you happy, my love?"

He takes my hand and placed it on his chest, directly over his heart. "More than anything else in the world, my Anna."

ABOUT JESSICA GRAYSON

Malak (wolf shifter) and Luna's story is next: **Protected By The Wolf Prince.**

If you enjoyed this book, please leave a review on Amazon and/or Goodreads.

Fairy Tale Retellings (Once Upon a Fairy Tale Romance Series)

Taken by the Dragon: A Beauty and the Beast Retelling

Captivated by the Fae: A Cinderella Retelling

Rescued By The Merman: A Little Mermaid Retelling

Bound To The Elf Prince: A Snow White Retelling

Claimed By The Bear King: A Snow Queen Retelling

Protected By The Wolf Prince: A Red Riding Hood Retelling

Do you like Dragon Shifters? Elves? Fae? Vampires?

Ice World Warrior Series

Claimed: Dragon Shifter Romance

Bound: Vampire Alien Romance

Rescued: Fae Alien Romance

Stolen: Werewolf Romance

Taken: Vampire Alien Romance

Fated: Dragon Shifter Romance

Want Dragon Shifters? You can dive into their world with this completed Duology.

Mosauran Series (Dragon Shifter Alien Romance)

The Edge of it All

Shape of the Wind

V'loryn Series (Vampire Alien Romance)
   Lost in the Deep End
   Beneath a Different Sky
   Under a Silver Moon

V'loryn Holiday Series (A Marek and Elizabeth Holiday novella takes place prior to their bonding)
   The Thing We Choose

V'loryn Fated Ones (Vampire Alien Romance)
   Where the Light Begins (Vanek's Story)

For information about upcoming releases Like me on
   Facebook at Jessica Grayson
   http://facebook.com/JessicaGraysonBooks.

ABOUT ARIA WINTER

Thank you so much for reading this. I hope you enjoyed this story. If you enjoy my writing, I also write under the pen name *Jessica Grayson*.

For information about upcoming releases Like me on Facebook (www.facebook.com/ariawinterauthor) or sign up for upcoming release alerts at my website:

Ariawinter.com

Want more Dragon Shifters? Check out my Beauty and the Beast Retelling below.

Once Upon A Fairy Tale Romance Series

Taken by the Dragon: A Beauty and the Beast Retelling

Captivated by the Fae: A Cinderella Retelling

Rescued By The Merman: A Little Mermaid Retelling

Bound to the Elf Prince: A Snow White Retelling

Elemental Dragon Warriors Series

Claimed by the Fire Dragon Prince

Stolen by the Wind Dragon Prince

Rescued by the Water Dragon Prince

Healed by the Earth Dragon Prince

Chosen By The Fire Dragon Guard

Saved By The Wind Dragon Guard

Treasured By The Water Dragon Guard

Taken By The Earth Dragon Guard

Cosmic Guardian Series

Charmed by the Fox's Heart

Seduced by the Peacock's Beauty

Protected by the Spider's Web